All my life the
couldn't see how
but now like Willy i'm free
and all i can see is they still wanna chase me
right down to Arizonee.
Now i aks ya,
i Sthat any way to treat a law-abiding doe-gee?
Respect to the max.
Word.

Get down to the bookshop

for more Bad Dog books!

Bad Dog and all that Hollywood HooHah

Bad Dog and Those Crazee Martians!

Bad Dog and the Curse of the President's Knee

Martin Chatterton

SCHOLASTIC

Scholastic Children's Books,
Commonwealth House, 1-19 New Oxford Street,
London, WC1A 1NU, UK
a division of Scholastic Ltd
London ~ New York ~ Toronto ~ Sydney ~ Auckland
Mexico City ~ New Delhi ~ Hong Kong

First published by Scholastic Ltd, 2003

ISBN 0 439 97954 4

Printed and bound by Nørhaven Paperback, Viborg, Denmark

10 9 8 7 6 5 4 3 2

CHAPTER 1

TONIGHT THERE'S GONNA BE A JAILBREAK

"WHO LET THE DOGS OUT? *WHO LET THE DOGS OUT?*"

I was only dimly aware of freaky Fester, the Undisputed Heavyweight ZitKing of the Universe, screaming below us as we cleared the perimeter wall, because I was clinging for dear life on to the neck of a flying robot-mutant-dog called Rover. My yard pal, The Most Righteous Reverend Bentley Sweetlord the Fourth, was right behind me, and we were trying real hard not to get in the way of Rover's ears as they rotated at two thousand revs per second, lifting us smoothly and silently up, up and away from Z-Block in the City Dog Pound. The sirens screamed down in the yard and we could make out the darkened figures of the guards scrambling around in blind panic.

Searchlights flickered into action and probed the dark corners of the exercise yard.

"Check out those suckers," chuckled Bentley into my ear. "The last thing they's lookin' for is a flyin' canine! Bad Dog, you weren't foolin': man, this bird can *fly*!"

He was right. Rover, a cross-bred android/ German Shepherd, the mutant result of a lunatic plot to overthrow the President (foiled by ME, naturally, tra-la), had been engineered well. His little motors purred silently as we rose into the night sky above the city, the only sound a soft disco chukka-wah chop made by Rover's ear rotors. Somehow he'd ended up back at the City Pound with me. He was operated by a special remote control gizmo I'd kept hold of and smuggled back into the Pound (don't ask how: the memory is painful enough; not to mention my rear end...).

Now two grizzled desperadoes (me and Bentley) were using Rover in a daring night-time jailbreak! Two dashing desperadoes who laughed (HA HA) in the face of dange—

Bentley poked me in the ribs with an elbow the size of a canoe and I snapped out of my daydream.

"OK, brother, where to?"

I hesitated for a moment. Our cunning plan only extended as far as getting clear of the Pound. Then it came to me, and I smiled back over my shoulder.

"The only place that tough guys like us head for when they're on the lam!" I growled in a low, masculine, movie-trailer voice-over kind of way.

I pointed south.

"Mexico!"

Hold up. What's all this about flying android dogs and jailbreaks and Presidents and all the rest of that freaky stuff?

OK. For those of you who've been spending the last few years on Mars, this is me:

Handsome li'l feller, ain't I? My name's Bad Dog, or at least that's what I get called most of the time, along with a bunch of other names, none of which I can repeat in polite company. Or yours either, for that matter, ha ha. The only important things you need to know about me are, in no particular order:

1. I'm a dog.

2. I'm not the kind of dog that people generally look at and decide to keep in their home as a treasured and valuable member of their family.

3. I've been in the slammer (otherwise known as Z-Block,) in the City Pound, three times.

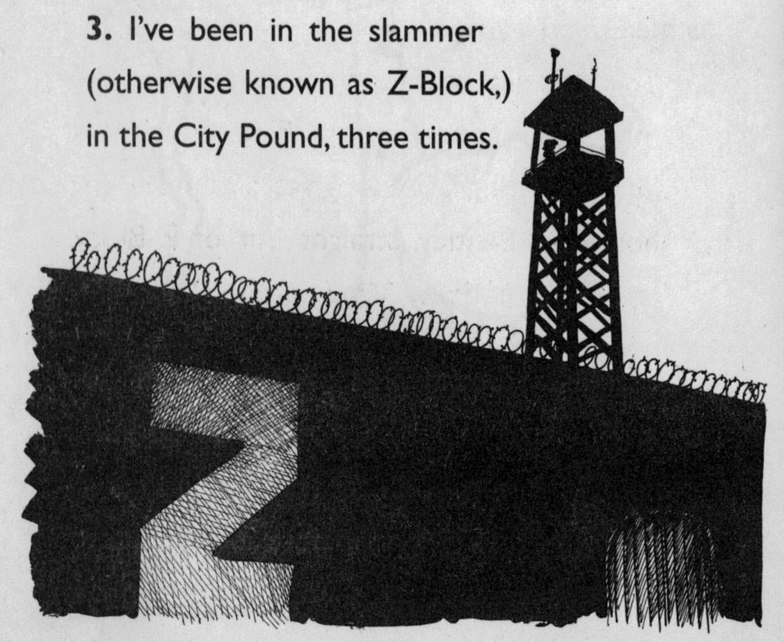

4. In the Pound, if you don't get picked out you get killed. You heard me.

5. The last three times I was about to get snuffed I miraculously got picked to be a famous Hollywood dog-star, then a member of the first mission to Mars and lastly, the latest doggy occupant of the White House. The First Dog, so to speak.

That last gig was where I met Rover, the mutant-dog dude, whose ears were now kindly rotating fast enough to lift me and my homeboy, Bentley, straight out of Z-Block and to freedom! Whoop whoop! Let's hear it for shady government scientific developments in robot technology! Cheers, applause, the crowd goes wild … YAAAAHHHH!

Oh, I nearly forgot. There's one more thing about me you need to know.

6. I *hate* cats. Yeah, yeah, I know. Those of you who followed my career closely, will know that at the White House my skin was saved by one Vernon Sangster, a member of the feline persuasion, and I should be cured of my lifelong hatred of all things cat.

But I'm not, OK? I *still* hate 'em and, by all that's doggy, I reserve my right to be prejudiced against the whiskery little freaks.

Which brings us up to date. If you need more detail you'll just have to look it all up. It's all there in the files.

OK. So where were we?

Mexico. Heading south of the border. On the lam from the man, down and dirty desperadoes, mean and magnificent. Breakin' rocks in the hot sun, I fought the law and the law won … but not this time! No sir, this time Bad Dog and The Reverend Bentley Sweetlord the Fourth are *gone*, man. Gone.

I lay back and relaxed as Bentley gave directions to Rover. We were high up now, and the sirens were just a distant blur somewhere out on the edge of my hearing. And I'm a dog, you understand, with super-doggy ears, which gives you some idea of how far we'd travelled. The stars looked great up here. We must have cut above the smog.

Bentley looked over at me.

"Mexico?"

"Yeah, Mexico. Like Butch Cassidy and the Sundown Kid," I murmured. "In that movie."

"That was Bolivia, numbnuts," said Bentley. "And it was the Sun*dance* Kid."

"Bolivia, shmolivia," I shot back, waving a paw in the air, airily. "It's all guacamole to me pardner. I know one thing though – Fester can't follow me all the way to Mexico."

"Fester can't, no," said Bentley. "But what about those guys?" He pointed a massive paw back past Rover's quivering ass-end.

I sat bolt upright, my heart jumping around like a landed fish.

Back behind us, about two miles distant, three black shapes had appeared. They were difficult to make out at first against the blue-black sky, but they were there all right. We could hear the steady thock-thock-thock of helicopter rotors. Big thock-thocks. The sight was a thock, I mean a shock.

"Probably just radio traffic reporters," I said,

the quaver in my voice doing a bad job of masking the healthy dose of cowardice that runs through me like custard in a doughnut.

A muffled boom came from the direction of the choppers and a white-hot fiery streak shot past us at the speed of light. It came close enough to singe my tail and exploded about fifty metres off our port side. We rocked violently in the air as the blast wave rolled over us.

"Yeah," said Bentley, rocking on his feet

"Probably just traffic reporters who upgraded their equipment to include air-to-air laser weaponry. In case they encounter a rival radio traffic reporter and have to engage them in mortal combat, I guess."

I've never appreciated sarcasm, unless it was me dishing it out, natch, and I was about to tell Bentley that, when another missile blazed past and exploded over our starboard side. This time I came within a whisker of falling off Rover when Bentley grabbed me by the ears and hauled me back on board.

"I never realized the City Dog Pound had that kind of fire-power," I yelped as the choppers launched a third strike. Bentley pushed Rover's head down and we went into a dive. The missile blazed harmlessly over us.

"It doesn't!" yelled Bentley. "Whoever's in those choppers ain't from the Pound. But can we save the discussion till later? We gotta get movin' bro'! Like, now."

Bentley looked around.

"You see a gas pedal anywhere?" he shouted above the noise of the wind rushing past us.

"Gas pedal?" I shouted back. "We're on a flyin' *dog*, dude! It hasn't got a gas pedal." I looked down and saw the ground racing towards us. Fast. "Besides, what we need right now is a brake pedal!"

Bentley leaned forward and spoke into Rover's ear.

"Can you go any faster?" he said.

Rover nodded and reached round to the back of his head. He pressed something under the fur and we shot forward like some kind of TV sci-fi hyperdrive special effect. Everything went blurry as it screamed past us. I howled and prepared to die as we shot towards the ground.

"Oh," said Bentley to Rover. "I forgot. Could we also not crash into the ground?"

Rover nodded and we levelled out just as a bone-shattering impact seemed inevitable. Rover's trailing leg knocked a TV satellite dish off a house roof and we rose back into the sky at supersonic speed.

"Man!" said Bentley, appreciatively to Rover. "They really did a number on you, brother!"

I didn't say anything. I was too busy whimpering and concentrating on not losing control of my bowel movements. My breathing gradually came back to normal and I began to relax a little. At the speed we were going, no chopper could keep pace. At least we'd lost those nasty missile-launching loons, and I said as much to Bentley.

He pointed over my shoulder. It took a minute to make out because Rover was vibrating like a demented blender, but after a moment I could see what he was pointing at.

It was the choppers.

Further back than they'd been, for certain. But still there, and keeping pace.

I turned back to Bentley. "Who *are* those guys?"

CHAPTER 2

MEN IN BLACK

Dawn broke somewhere over the Mojave desert, and red shadows raced below as the sun came up ahead of us. We'd been flying for the past hour and hadn't seen the chopper posse for the last thirty minutes or so. My breathing was deep and resonant as per usual. In fact I could, technically, be described as being asleep. Like all dogs, I sleep with one eye open, to check on stuff.

A judder shook me awake and in no more than

a couple of minutes I got both eyes fully operational. As I woke I became aware that Rover was bumping around like a cork on the high seas, in a way that caused me to re-examine my reasons for escaping from Z-Block.

"What's happening?" I said to Bentley, who was busy licking his butt.

"Hmm?" he said, absently, his mind still fixed on his morning wash.

"Those bumps," I said. "What gives?"

Bentley lifted his head from between his knees and took a look around through hooded lids.

"Turbulence, dude. Relax."

As he spoke, Rover gave a shudder and coughed. It was a nasty, deep, wet cough that sounded as though something important had broken loose inside him and was rattling around. We lurched to the right and almost stopped in mid-air. There was a moment's silence and then Rover chugged forward again.

I was about to breathe a sigh of relief when my nostrils twitched. "Can you smell burning?" I said, a trifle nervously.

Bentley sniffed. "Yeah, now you come to mention it, I can."

I twisted my head this way and that, looking for something on the ground that might be the cause: a campfire perhaps, a carelessly discarded cigarette, anything. But we were too high for anything like that to reach us. Then I spotted the source of the smoke and my stomach lurched.

"HIS ASS IS ON FIRE!" I screamed, in an embarrassing high-pitched squeal. "Rover's ass! It's on fire!"

It was. As we looked on, horrified, a thick plume of black smoke streamed out of Rover's rear end and we juddered to a halt.

"Uh-oh," said Bentley. "That's not good." A bid for understatement of the year, in my opinion.

I didn't get time to sneer out a sarcastic reply. I was too busy screaming as Rover went into a steep nosedive. A noise like a jet engine digesting a man-size toolbox was coming from somewhere deep inside the flying mutant-dog and the desert floor started getting real close. I grabbed hold of Rover's remote and frantically began pressing buttons. Nothing happened.

Bentley, standing up on Rover's back like some demented surf-dog, seemed to be taking things a little too lightly for my liking. I was about to yell at him to do something useful when I realized that was exactly what he was doing. He was surfing Rover.

"Li'l somethin' I picked up out on the coast!" he shouted. Bentley shifted his weight and Rover began to level out. He was still bucking around more than I liked, but at least we weren't hurtling towards the desert at the speed of light any more.

Bentley pointed towards a big sand dune we could see up ahead. "I'm gonna try and set us down over there!" he shouted. "Hold on!"

This last bit didn't need to be said. I was already holding on so tight it was touch-and-go whether Rover didn't die from strangulation before we hit the deck. I had put the remote control between my teeth so that I could hold on more tightly.

"Here we go!" yelled Bentley as the dune loomed up in front of us. We hit the top of the dune and bounced, almost tossing me off Rover's back. We came back down on to the downslope of the dune in a great shower of sand and dust.

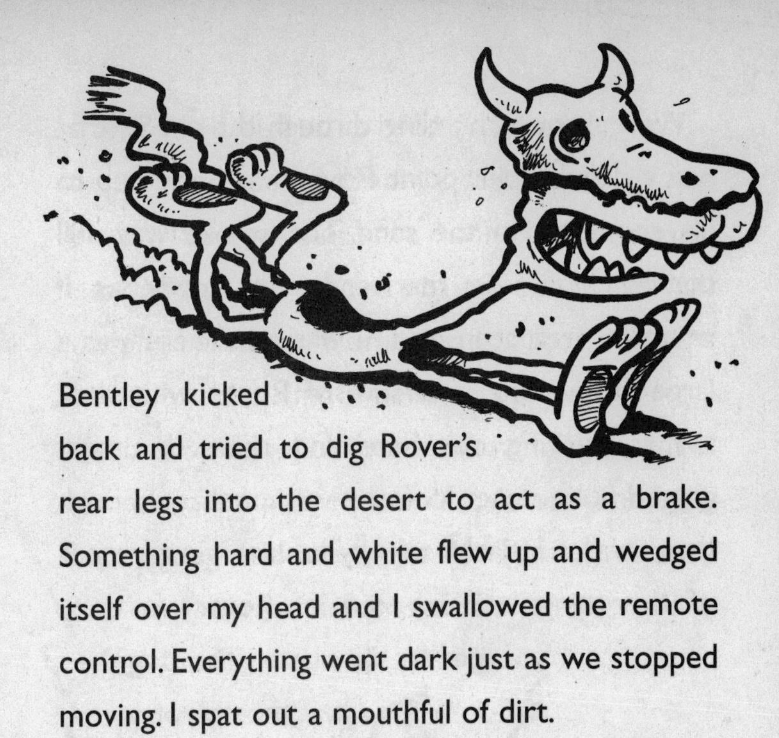

Bentley kicked back and tried to dig Rover's rear legs into the desert to act as a brake. Something hard and white flew up and wedged itself over my head and I swallowed the remote control. Everything went dark just as we stopped moving. I spat out a mouthful of dirt.

"I'm blind!" I wailed. "Blind, I tell you! BLI-HI-HI-IIIINNNNNNDDDDD!"

A huge paw reached over and tugged a skeletal cattle head off me. Bentley looked down at me, a pitying expression on his face.

"For cryin' out loud, brother, show a little backbone."

I tried to laugh it off as a jolly jape but Bentley wasn't listening.

I looked around.

We'd stopped hurtling through the air. So that was a definite plus point. Rover was buried up to his shoulders in the sand. The smoke was still coming from his rear end, but slowly, as if whatever had been on fire was out. There was a large gash along one side of Rover with dark shapes sticking out here and there. I almost gagged, but a closer look showed me that although there was a little bit of icky-looking gunge, most of the things sticking out of Rover were metallic or plastic. The dog was mostly robot.

Bentley, who was standing near Rover's head, looked at me and shook his own head from side to side. He reached down and softly closed Rover's eyes; one old soldier to another.

I choked back a sob, even though, to be honest, Rover had been a royal pain in the ass back when he was a proper dog. Even as a mutant android he was something of a goon. But, he *was* still a dog, right? *And* he'd just helped us skip jail.

I perked back up and began to take a look around.

The first thing I noticed was a whole lot of nothing. Every direction I looked revealed more nothing. Just sand. Lots and lots of sand rising and falling away into the distance. It was like being on the bottom of the ocean. Except for the total absence of water, obviously. Some scraggy looking hills wobbled in the heat about a kilometre away. It was only a few minutes past sunrise and we were already cooking like a pair of hot dogs on a griddle.

"OK," I said. "We better get moving."

Bentley was shaking his head. "Uh-uh," he grunted. "We hafta bury this brother. It's the only decent thing to do."

"Bury him?" I looked across at the gigantic robot dog slumped on the sand. "Have you noticed the size of that sucker? We'd need a team of qualified miners and a couple of bulldozers to get him halfway covered. And, in case you hadn't noticed we're in the middle of a des..."

I stopped after Bentley gave me The Look. Lesser dogs have spontaneously exploded after being given one of Bentley's Looks. I was made of sterner stuff, but I still knew when to quit.

"OK, OK," I said, holding up my paw. "We'll bury him."

It took most of the morning to dig a hole big enough to get Rover into. If Bentley hadn't had paws like dump-truck shovels it would've taken till next Christmas, but eventually we got him decently covered up. We made a little marker from a coupla pieces of wood and the bleached white cattle skull. Looked quite good in a kind of cheesy south-western kind of way. The Reverend Bentley said a few short words over the grave while I did my best to breathe.

The temperature was off the scale by now. I don't know if you've ever been out on a really, really hot day and thought "man, this is really hot"? Well, imagine the heat being twice that PLUS you're wearing a fur coat you can't take off AND you've been digging in the dirt for the last six hours, and you'll get a rough idea of how I felt. Bentley didn't seem affected at all. It was as though his street cool was acting like some sort of Power Shield.

Myself, I was panting like a small tyre with a big nail in it. I needed water and shade and rest, in that order.

Bentley finished the service and looked over at me.

"We better go," he said.

"Oh, *now* you wanna go?" I gasped. "What's the big rush? Maybe we should bury the rest of the cow?" I pointed to the cattle bones on the sand.

"Well, you stay, brother," said Bentley. "Me, I'm goin' before those dudes get here." He pointed across the desert.

On the horizon, a thick cloud of dust was moving in our direction. I might have thought it was just that, a dust-cloud, if it wasn't for the faint sound of engine noise.

"Do you think it's those same guys?" I said.

"I'm not waitin' around to find out," said Bentley. "Let's see if we can make those hills." He nodded. I gathered all my strength (which took about two seconds; there wasn't a whole lot of it there to begin with...) and we vamoosed across the dunes towards the hills.

They were a lot further than we'd thought, and we weren't vamoosing as quickly as we needed to if we were going to make into the hills before whatever was in the dust-cloud arrived at our crash site. But just over the top of a particularly big dune we came across some weird rock formations rising up into little towers and canyons. It wasn't the Hollywood Hilton but there was shade(!) and we clambered gratefully up and into a cave-like hollow at the top of one of the stone towers.

We flopped down, our noses draped over the lip of the cave entrance, and looked out across the desert, back towards where we'd come from.

Bentley had fashioned a field telescope from the trunk of a hollowed-out cactus and some highly polished flat stones bound with strips of leaves we'd plaited into twine. Only kidding; what do you think we are? Special Doggy Forces? Nah, we just screwed up our eyes and squinted into the sun. The dust-cloud had settled revealing a strange, large-wheeled vehicle. It was painted in desert camouflage. Four people jumped down and stood looking at the grave containing our dear departed Rover.

"They're probably just after Rover," I said. "I'll bet those guys are nothing to do with the Pound at all. It's just the military checking on a bit of missing kit."

Bentley grunted. It was one of those grunts you could take either way. I took it as agreement with my new theory and was about to expand in this direction when the group of figures turned and started looking in our direction. I leaped back into the cave.

"They've seen us!" I yelped.

Bentley hadn't moved. "No, we're too far away brother. It's gotta be something else."

"Yeah, yeah," I stuttered. "Some kind of white-hot secret radar tracking technology that can spot runaway pooches across three miles of desert scrub..."

"I don't think that's what hipped them on to us, brother," said Bentley, looking skywards.

I trotted back outside the cave and followed his gaze. Wheeling in long, lazy circles dead above us were six or seven huge birds. Big, long-necked, black-winged birds with curved beaks and harsh, cruel, yellow eyes (I was imagining that last bit, my eyes aren't that good). Vultures.

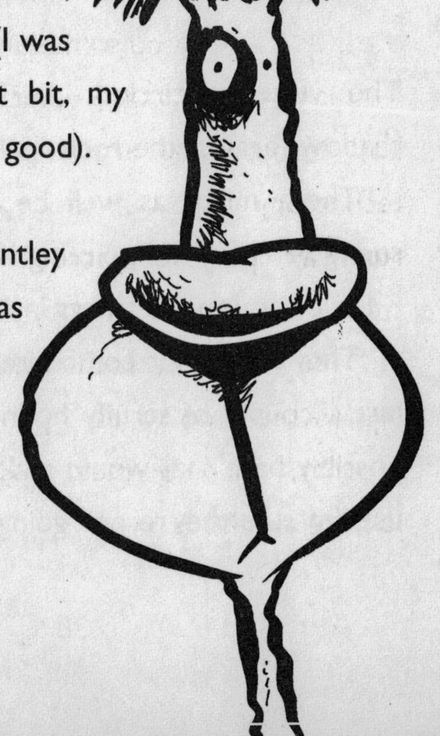

I looked at Bentley and gulped. This was turning out to be a bad day.

Chapter 3

Jump Around

The vultures circled overhead casting long shadows against the rock walls of the canyon.

"There might as well be a big neon arrow saying *here they are* pointing at us," said Bentley.

I tried to look at things in a positive light.

"They might not come after us," I said. "We're just a couple of scruffy hounds. What could we possibly have that would make them come after us? I'm *sure* they're not going to come after us.

There's just no way they're coming after us."

Bentley was squinting through the heat shimmer.

"They're coming after us," he said.

"Curses!" I yelled. Actually I said something a bit stronger than that: you'll have to just imagine what you'd yell if you were stuck in the middle of the baking hot desert, on the run from a relentless secret military force, there were ravenous vultures eyeing you up as potential breakfast material *and* you were really thirsty. It'd probably be a little bit stronger than "curses" (which no one in the history of the universe has ever used in real life).

Anyway, where was I?

Oh yeah: those guys were *still* after us. I summoned up all my reserves of street cool and demonstrated how to act in a crisis by running round the cave in little circles and yelling in a high-pitched voice. Works for me every time.

"Whaddawedowhaddawedowhaddawedo? Whaddawedo?" I squeaked.

On my third circuit Bentley slapped me across the chops and I bounced off a large rock.

"Pull yourself together, dog!" he barked, bringing me to my senses. "There's only one thing we can do: we run!"

I gave a last hopeful glance in the direction of our pursuers, wondering if maybe they'd decided to call it a day and head back home to their underground lair, or wherever it was they called home. They hadn't. The cloud of dust was heading our way at about a bazillion miles an hour.

Bentley yanked my collar and dragged me out of the cave. We scrambled down the side of the rock formation towards the desert floor.

Once outside the cave the temperature rose. It was probably no higher than the temperature on the surface of the sun, say, but plenty hot for this pooch. I was turning into a walking chilli dog.

I broke out into a sweat immediately and then remembered that dogs don't sweat and had to content myself with panting. I mean, who designed dogs? Not anyone who lived in a desert, that's for sure. Big fur coat, no sweat glands. As we trotted across the burning sand I thought about weeping but I didn't have enough moisture in me to muster a decent tear.

Bentley didn't seem troubled and lolloped along like a big hairy air-conditioned cruise ship. I needed a drink and I needed it now. I remembered somewhere seeing a TV programme about desert survival.

The guy in it, all done up in nice khakis, had got water from a cactus plant.

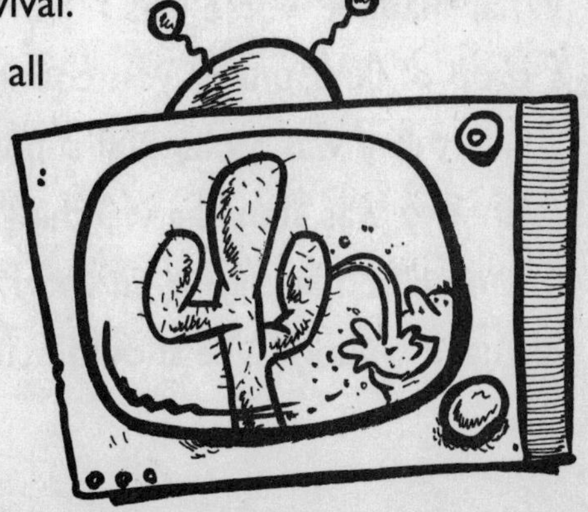

The water had been clear and clean, like he'd just ordered a bottle of iced mineral water from hotel room service. We passed a patch of cactus and I decided to give it a try. I picked a nice juicy-looking one and sank my teeth into it.

They probably heard my screams on the moon as I took a big mouthful of needle-sharp spikes.

Somehow I'd forgotten about the spikes. What made it worse was I didn't get so much as a drop of fluid, unless you counted the blood, of which there was a plentiful supply.

Bentley was standing watching me.

"You all done playing *Survivor*?" he said, shaking his head wearily. "We should make for the hills."

He gestured up ahead at the brown shapes on the horizon. I estimated the distance to the mountains to be about five thousand miles. They were wobbling like jello in the waves of heat rising from the baked desert floor.

"It's too far," I whimpered, spitting cactus spikes out. "We'll never make it that far. They'll catch us!"

"Hell," said Bentley. "That doesn't matter. We'll be dead from the heat long before we get to the hills."

"Oh," I said. "That's all right then." And we trotted on.

I risked a glimpse over my shoulder. The cloud was still there. It had probably taken the posse a few minutes to track where we were, but now they were headed towards us, no mistake. The hills were getting no closer and I was about to just lie down and surrender when I heard a strange rumbling sound. At first I thought it was the engine noise from the posse at our heels, but then I realized it was something else.

"Listen!" I gasped to Bentley.

"What?" he said, irritably.

"That noise," I said. "I know what that is! It's water, dude! Water!"

Bentley slowed down a little and looked at me as if I was a certifiable loon.

"Man, you're hearing things," he said. "It's a mirage. Out in the desert you imagine all sorts of things, like ice cream and castles … and water."

He was about to say something more when his ears pricked up. "Funny," he said. "I'm gettin' that mirage comin' through too."

In front of us the sand and scrub rose upwards on a low rise, obscuring whatever lay ahead. We trotted forward and came to a rapid halt as the ground fell away from us. We were standing on the edge of a huge canyon cut deep through the desert. The opposite edge of the canyon stood about seventy metres from us.

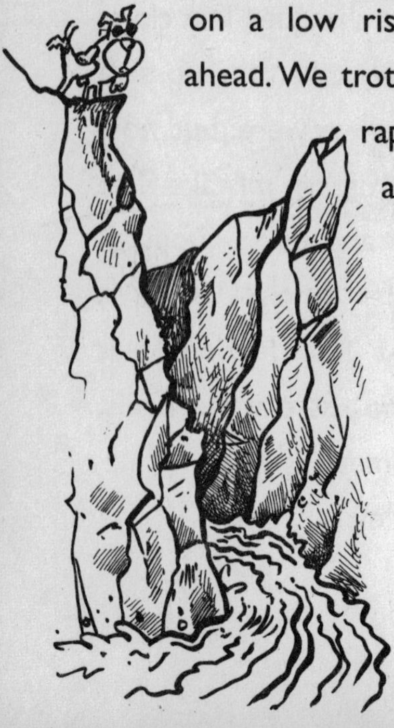

The walls of the canyon were sheer and smooth, falling about seventy metres to a river racing through, fast and deep and wet.

"See!" I yelled triumphantly. "Water! Told ya!"

Bentley nodded. He didn't seem as excited as me by the discovery of the water. He looked back. The dust-cloud was a lot nearer now and we could make out the shape of the vehicle barrelling towards us.

I was leaning out over the edge of the canyon, looking down.

"What are doing?" said Bentley.

I looked at him.

"We can make it," I said.

"What do you mean 'make it'?" said Bentley. "You aren't thinking about jumpin', are you, brother?"

"Sure," I said, nodding like one of those dumb toy nodding dogs. I looked at the posse. "Besides, what choice do we have?"

"We fight," said Bentley, turning towards the dust-cloud.

"Fight? What with? You gonna…"

Bentley cut me off in mid-sentence. "Don't you get it brother? I can't swim!"

I laughed, probably the only time anyone's laughed at the Reverend and lived.

"Hell, you probably won't need to swim. The fall's gonna kill ya!" As I said it I got a strange feeling of dejà vu but I didn't have time to worry about it. The chasers were very close now. Their vehicle skidded to a halt about thirty metres away and four big, scary-lookin' dudes in black combat gear dropped out. One carried a net and one a length of rope. The other two had hold of mighty-looking tranquillizer guns. At least I hoped they were tranquillizer guns.

Bentley looked across at me and shrugged.

"I seen this movie too," he said and winked.

"Whoo-hoo!" I yelled and we walked towards the posse, our paws in the air. They relaxed and, as they did, we turned and sprinted for the edge of the canyon.

"WHAAA
AAAAAAOO
OOOOOOOOOOOOOOOO
OOOOOOOOOOOOOOOO
OOOHHHHH!!!" we screamed together as we leaped out into space, our legs windmilling and ears trailing out as we fell. As I got twisted around in mid-air, I caught a split-second glimpse of four heads peering over the edge as we fell away from them, down towards the roiling water.

Chapter 4

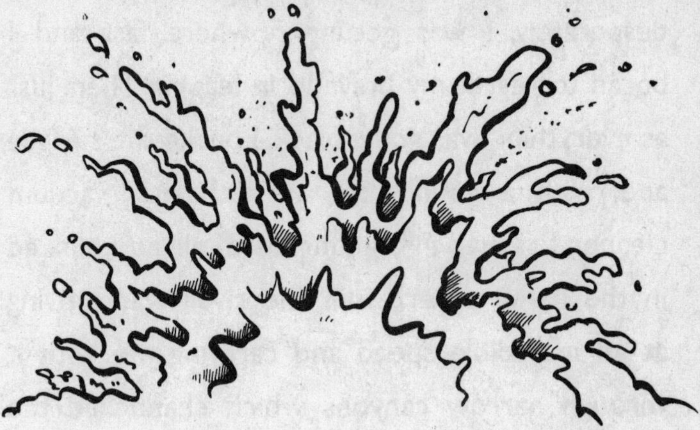

Midday at the Oasis

The river rose to meet us and we smashed down into the racing torrent like two hairy meteorites crashing to earth. All the breath was knocked out of me and I sank like a stone, the current pushing me deeper and deeper underwater. I tried to drink myself to the surface and sucked down the icy water in great gulps until I realized this plan had a downside: drowning. I switched to Plan B and started swimming.

I thrashed upwards, banging my head on rocks as the river raced along the canyon floor. Paddling desperately, I was getting nowhere fast and I began to regret my bravado in leaping. Then, just as everything was going black, I broke the surface and, with a sound like an asthmatic vacuum cleaner, I gasped in big lungfuls of air and blinked in the harsh desert sun. The river was moving at an incredible speed and carrying me with it through narrow canyons which channelled the tonnes of water through a natural rollercoaster of rock and sand. It was all I could do to stay above the surface, bobbing along like a hairy cork. I couldn't see Bentley anywhere. I tried to shout but the deafening roar of the water carooming off the canyon drowned out all other sounds.

Then, about six metres away, the river erupted as if ten tonnes of dynamite had exploded just beneath the surface and Bentley popped out of the water. For a dog that couldn't swim he was doing a great impression of an dolphin: I swear that for a second or two he tail-walked along the river surface.

He saw me and then flipped upside down, his ass-end poking out above the water. I paddled across and hauled him upright, with some difficulty. Forgetting all about being cool we clung to each other like big soppy puppies as we raced along. We must have stayed like that for twenty minutes, getting colder and colder. In the middle of the baking desert we were gonna die of cold.

My teeth were chattering and I was about to suggest we swam for the bank when I realized that we were slowing down. We rounded a bend and the canyon walls fell away revealing a wide open stretch of water. The ebb and flow of the river gradually carried us into a quiet shallow area of large boulders and stones where our feet could touch the bed. We clambered out and flopped, exhausted, on to a large flat rock, like two landed fish. After a while our teeth stopped chattering.

Bentley looked at me and we burst out laughing.

"Whoo-ee man," said Bentley. "I guess The Reverend *can* swim, after all!" He rocked back and forth, laughing like a drain. S'funny that expression; personally, I've never heard a drain make any kind of a laugh, not so much as a giggle.

We looked around and saw that the canyon had opened out into a kind of valley, still the desert but with a little more vegetation, particularly close to the water. After a while we stood up and started to think about what to do. There was no sign of our pursuers.

"I guess we lost them," I said.

Bentley looked around.

"Maybe," he said. "But those birds are still hangin' around. *They* still think we're lunch."

I looked up to see the now familiar shape of the vultures wheeling overhead. I threw a stone at them but, since they were about five miles high, I missed. The mention of lunch had reminded me how hungry I was. I looked at Bentley and licked my chops.

"What you lookin' at, brother?" said the Reverend. "I'm not sure I like the expression on your face. Don't be gettin' any ideas about snackin' on my hindquarters; not if you want to continue breathing."

"What?" I said innocently. "I was just..."

"I know exactly what you was jus' doin'," said Bentley. "Now quit it and let's see if we can figure something out." He looked up.

"If we can still see those birds I reckon whoever's chasin' us can too," said Bentley, pointing out the obvious and doing zilch to help cheer me up. I was just about to snap back a nasty quip when I heard music. It sounded pretty close, too.

Bentley had heard it as well, but had a look on his face like he didn't want to believe it. I scampered up the rest of the river bank and stood on the crest of a small rise and almost fainted with joy. Below us lay a glittering tropical oasis. A sparkling blue pool, overhung with picture-perfect palms, shimmered and flickered in the sun while ochre-coloured camels lazily blinked in the shade. To one side of the pool three bikini-clad women splashed and shouted in the water while a muscular guy wearing plenty of gold and holding a microphone did a crazy kind of dance on the shore. A cosmadelic thumping bass beat throbbed across the sand towards us.

I grabbed hold of Bentley.

"Are you seein' this?" I asked him.

He nodded and then shook his head.

"Well?" I said. "Which is it? Do you see it or not?"

"I see it, brother," said Bentley. "I just don't straight out believe it. It's one of them mirages I was tellin' you about."

"Mirage? Since when do mirages get down like that?" I twitched my rear end in syncopation with the music. I don't mind telling you, despite the hunger and thirst and all round exhaustion I was getting jiggy wid it – I was putting on the *dog*.

Bentley looked at me sadly. "Man, who told you you could dance? That's plain nasty."

I wasn't listening. I was too busy funkin' on down. With a twist and a spin I headed down the slope towards the oasis yapping along in time to the beat. Bentley followed behind, shouting at first but then kinda gettin' into it

and shakin' his righteous booty alongside yours truly. We tumbled down the hill and rolled right up to the water's edge. We jumped up and began shaking our tails in time to the music. I noticed that there were quite a lot of other people I hadn't noticed before. None of them were smiling.

The music stopped.

Everyone looked at us.

"What the BLEEP BLEEEP the BLEEP are those two BLEEP doing on my BLEEPER BLEEP BLEEP shoot?" shouted the guy who'd been singing. "Get them the BLEEP BLEEP outta my BLEEP BLEEP face! Fluff Booty has spoken!"

"I don't think he likes us," I said in a whisper to Bentley.

"No kiddin', Sherlock."

"And what kind of a name is 'Fluff'?"

The muscular dude was still ranting so I sat down on a nearby rock and waited for him to run out of steam. The rock I was sitting on collapsed like it was made of cardboard. I looked at it. It *was* made of cardboard. I looked around. Now I was up close and personal with the oasis I could see that everything was not as it seemed. The palm trees, for example, were made of plywood, propped up at the back with lengths of raw lumber. The water itself *was* actually water but a little probing revealed it was sitting on a huge sheet of blue plastic set into the sand. I nudged Bentley to alert him to my discoveries.

In the background Fluff Booty was still bleeping away and making strange motions with his arms. His fingers were extended towards us and he kept shrugging and pointing. Various other people flapped around him.

"Do you know what's goin' on?" I asked Bentley.

"Nope," said Bentley out of the side of his mouth. "But I know one thing; if that noisy sucker doesn't quit yappin' he's gonna get a special sermon from The Reverend."

I nodded. Fluff Booty was giving me a headache too and was showing no signs of falling quiet.

Bentley threw back his head and barked.

It was like the roar of a Tyrannosaurus Rex booming out across some prehistoric swamp-type place (except we were in the desert). As the last howling bass notes of the bark reverberated around the oasis, everything went silent.

Fluff Booty looked over the top of his shades and thought about saying something. Then he looked a bit closer at Bentley and decided against it. Instead he pulled a white and gold fur robe around his shoulders and turned his back on us.

The robe had "Fluff" picked out in diamonds across the shoulders. I noticed with revulsion that an assistant thrust a fluffy white cat, wearing a large diamond collar, into his arms. Fluff tickled it under its disgusting fat white chin and kissed it. It was all I could do to keep myself from puking on the spot.

"I'll be in my BLEEP BLEEPIN' trailer," yelled Fluff. "Y'all straighten this BLEEPIN' BLEEP mess up!"

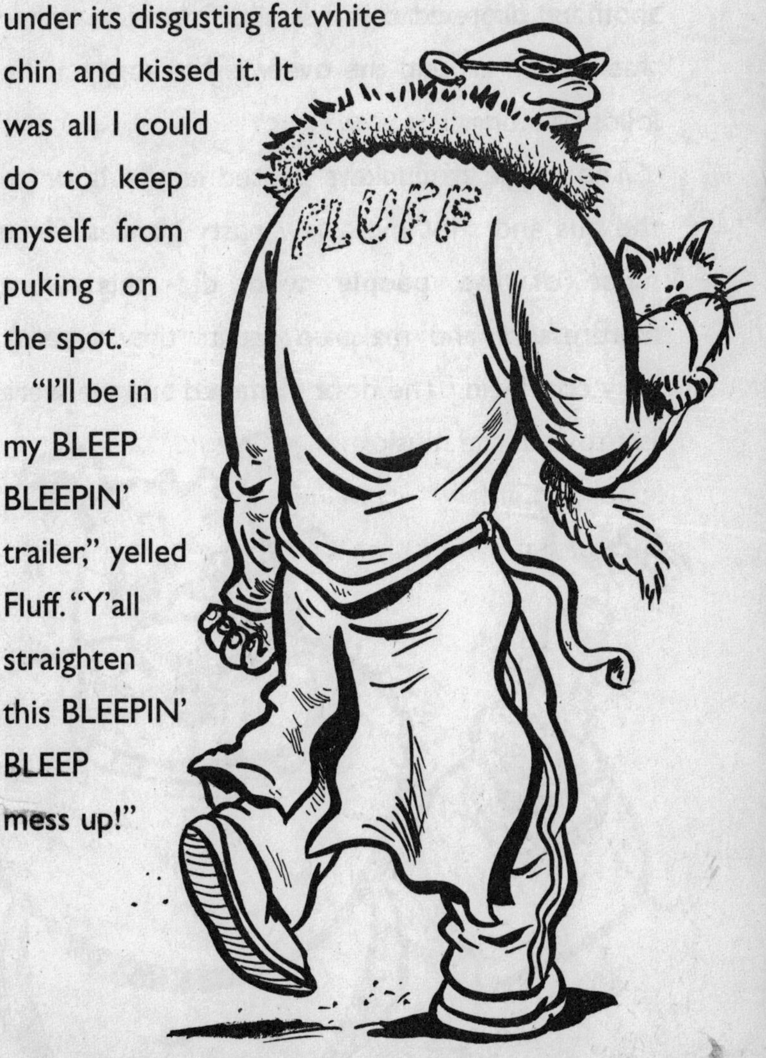

Trailed by a small army of hangers-on, he rolled his way towards a sleek silver bus parked about thirty metres away. I noticed he walked kinda funny, with one arm stuck straight down and one shoulder dropped towards the floor. The other was tucked around the overweight moggy as he lolloped along.

The gaggle of flunkeys paused at the door to the bus and shot me a few nasty glances. Since most of the people who did this were hairdressers and make-up artists they weren't very convincing. The door slammed and we were left to face the music.

Chapter 5

Bow Wow Wow Yippee Oh Yippee Ay

There was a moment's silence as everyone looked at us like we'd dropped out of the sky (which we had, when you come to think about it), and then they all turned away and got on with what they were doing. All except two huge guys wearing a lot of gold jewellery and one skinny dude who was wearing a large set of earphones and standing behind a complicated bit of equipment. The three of them had been off to one side giggling like a bunch of schoolkids through the whole thing. Now they ambled over to us.

"Man," said the skinny guy, shaking his head from side to side. "That was the bomb! Woo!"

He knocked fists together with one of the big guys, who was shaking with laughter.

I started to explain but they just carried on laughing like drains.

"You see his face, bro'?" said one of the big dudes. He was wearing a hockey shirt the size of Nebraska. "Jes' gettin' into his thang, when, whammo, Scoobs and Scrappy-doo here roll into town! He jes' 'bout BLEEP the big mouth BLEEP!"

And with that they all doubled up again. We

waited patiently while they recovered. I passed the time by watching the rolls of blubber vibrate as the big dudes laughed.

The skinny guy bent down till he was face to face with me.

"You his agent?" he said, jerking a thumb at Bentley.

The big dudes doubled over again. This was getting boring so Bentley pushed one of them over and did his Big Bark thing again.

This time, instead of laughing, the skinny dude just looked at the two big guys and said, "*That's* what we need!"

He trotted back to the pile of equipment and lugged out a big tape recorder and microphone.

"My name's Phones," he said, twiddling with the controls. "These two underdeveloped fellas are Slim and Shady. The one sittin' on his ass is Slim. Other one's Shady. They's brothers. Like real brothers: twins, in fac'."

Slim and Shady nodded towards us. It didn't seem to worry them that they were talking to dogs.

Phones set the recorder down on the sand and thrust the microphone towards Bentley.

"Now I know you is just a dog and all," he said. "But do you think you could give me that bark one more time?"

Bentley looked at him and then over at me. He raised a quizzical eyebrow.

"Can't hurt none," I said. "Let 'er rip, buddy."

Once more Bentley barked. The dials on the front of the tape recorder slammed up against the red markings and Phones ripped the headset off and started yelling something about his mother. I think.

"That was great, man!" he said. I felt a bit left out so I gave a bark too.

Phones gave me a look. "Yeah, dude," he said, nodding. "We can use that too. Gives me a bit of hi-lo to play off."

I didn't have a clue what he was talking about but it sounded pretty nice so I just sat there smiling. Slim and Shady were smiling too. We were all so happy I could have burst into song except that we were still being followed by a bunch of psycho government creepoids. Plus, I was tired. And hungry. Very hungry.

Suddenly a waft of cooked meat came drifting across the desert air and I almost fainted. Bentley caught it too and we twitched our noses in the direction it was coming from. Phones looked at us.

"You guys hungry?"

We nodded weakly.

"I'll take that as a yes," said Phones. He pointed off in the direction of the smell. "Catering truck's right over there. Go he'p yourse..."

He broke off in mid-sentence because he was talking to fresh air. At the mention of the word "catering", me and Bentley had high-tailed it at the speed of sound in the direction of the truck.

Spread out on a white table was a feast: fried chicken, fresh grilled T-bone steak, all the food a dog could want. We wasted no time and in a nano-second most of the tastiest portions were nestling snugly inside our bloated stomachs. The table looked like a plague of locusts had stripped it bare.

We lay on our backs in the shade of the catering truck and gazed up at the desert sky contented. For a few happy minutes we forgot all about being on the run from a relentless black-clad posse of mysterious government spooks. I closed my eyes.

Our peace was shattered by an ungodly noise

coming from near the oasis. It was a dog barking. I'd recognize the sound anywhere.

"Hey!" I said. "There's another dog here!"

The bark came again but this time it seemed to be cut off in mid-woof with a scratchy howl. Then it was repeated, then cut short again.

"Man," said Bentley, his eyes wide. "Sounds like that pooch is gettin' a whuppin'."

We had just formed a quick plan to surgically enter the area and perform a Special Forces style doggy rescue when a long bass note dropped in behind the barking.

"You know," said the Reverend. "That bark sounds kinda familiar."

Now he mentioned it, the sound was ringing a few bells with me too. Then the penny dropped. The bark was Bentley's bark!

We trotted over in the direction of the noise. Back over by the fake oasis, Phones, Slim and Shady were gathered round a mixing desk. Two enormous speakers were booming out a series of beats mixed in with Bentley's bark. Then came another, slightly higher-pitched bark over the top. It sounded like some whiny little poodle with an asthma problem was coughing up a big ball of six-week-old cat fur. It was horrible. Then, with a jolt, I realized it was me making the sound. My bark! I reassessed the sound and found that I'd been mistaken about how bad it sounded. Now I had a chance to listen, and with the knowledge that it was my bark, it really sounded pretty good.

Behind the desk, Phones bobbed and weaved, his long arms flicking and scratching as he tweaked switches and flipped large round, black objects on two turntables. In front, Slim and Shady, holding big microphones upside down, ducked and swayed in time to the beat. They began rapping, flinging their arms out in front of them and grabbing their privates. (Not each other's privates, you understand, just their own. I assumed it was some sort of human thing, but who am I to get all hoity-toity? I'm a dog: we sniff butts.)

I couldn't make out many of the words and those I could understand would have brought a blush to my cheeks if dogs were able to blush, which they can't. But the beat was infectious and me and Bentley started groovin' right along.

Eventually it all came to an end and the three performers slapped high fives and butted their heads together (not hard, just kind of friendly). They were still congratulating each other when the door to the bus flew open and Fluff Booty stood there, his oiled muscles quivering. A couple of flunkeys stood behind him, arms crossed and lips pouting. The cat just sat there, as cats do, looking as dumb as a fence-post.

"What the BLEEP is BLEEP goin' down an' BLEEP? Will you sorry-ass BLEEP BLEEPS get the BLEEP back on track and deliver some BLEEP for me to work with? I'm a BLEEP artist! I gotta have some peace round heah, ya trash BLEEPS! You wan' I slap ya upside yo' head an' BLEEP, y'all?"

Slim moved quicker than I would have believed possible for a guy who looked like he regularly snacked on whole roast oxen and fried hippo steaks. He was up to the door of the bus before Fluff Booty had time to move. Slim grabbed him by the front of his white vest and lifted him clean off his heels, muscles or no muscles.

He dropped the cat who miaowed and scuttled back into the bus.

"Cleopatra! Darling!" Fluff Booty squealed in a very embarrassing manner. His voice sounded different. "Unhand me instantly, you overgrown delinquent!" squeaked Fluff in a cut-glass English accent. He sounded like that actor, whassisname? Huge Grunt or something. "You may have injured Cleopatra, you lout! My agent has absolutely forbidden you from approaching me in this uncouth and surly manner! I'm going to count to te—"

Slim raised a mighty paw and slapped Fluff Booty firmly on the outside of his head. Fluff Booty fell quiet.

"Don't get carried away wi' yo'sef, brother," rumbled Slim in a voice like distant thunder. "Don' forget who you is talking to. Have some respec' for some real brothers, y'hear? Now go back in yo' li'l trailer and lift some o' those pretty li'l pastel-coloured weights you keep back there 'fore I decide to bury yo' ass out here."

A little wiry guy wearing a black suit raced across and spoke soothingly to Slim in a broad Scottish accent.

"Hey, big fella, relax, relax. C'mon, put him down."

Slim looked at the little guy.

"That's right," said the little guy. "Nice and easy. You know it makes sense."

"OK, Freddie," said Slim. "But you keep this sorry excuse outta my face, y'hear?"

Slim dropped Fluff Booty to the floor and stalked off back to the mixing desk. Freddie hustled Fluff back up into the bus and closed the doors.

Bentley looked thoughtfully at the bus.

"That Fluff guy is beginning to bug me," he said.

Chapter 6

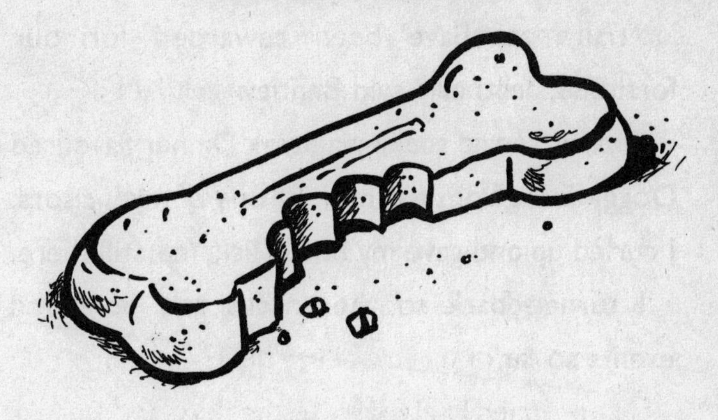

Scooby Snacks

Bentley and I sank back gratefully into the soft, fat, leopard-skin printed cushions on the Phatphreak Crew Tour Bus as we watched the desert landscape slip by outside the tinted windows. It was frosty air-conditioned cool inside and we stretched sleepily as the bus picked up speed. Freddie, the little wiry guy, who turned out to be the Phatphreak Crew manager, had managed to rustle up a box of Premier Doggy Treats from somewhere and we passed them back and forth between us as we travelled south.

"Truly we have been rewarded for our fortitude, brother!" said Bentley.

"Amen," I said sucking a Steak Dinner flavoured Doggy Treat from the back of one of my incisors. I curled up and gave my butt a lick. Yep, still there.

I turned back to the snacks and pondered events so far.

Things had moved pretty quick since the jailbreak. The crash, the chase, the desert heat and now this.

Phones, Slim and Shady, who were asleep on the other side of the bus, had explained that they were the fabulous Phatphreak Crew, an up-and-coming hardcore rapping outfit straight outta Los Angeles. It was beginning to happen for them: lots of press coverage, some good record sales, plenty of sell-out gigs. The only problem was that the bigger they got, the more big-headed Fluff Booty had become.

"Fluff Booty!" said Phones, and he'd spat on to the thick, purple shag pile carpet that hugged almost all surfaces of the bus that weren't covered in gold lamé, or sequin-spangled crushed velvet.

"I wouldn't min' so much 'cept the sucker's not even from the 'hood! He's a *ballet dancer*! An' he's *English*. When was the last time one-a-them uptight, umbrella-totin', fish-and-chip-munchin', floppy-haired Hugh Grant dudes really cut loose and got down?"

It had been Scots Freddie who'd hooked up Fluff with the Phatphreak Crew. The Crew needed Fluff as a pretty-boy front man, he needed them for their music and street cool.

Freddie, who'd been in the music biz since before the Dawn of Time, had put it all together. Now, when it was all happening for them, tempers were beginning to fray as Fluff Booty started to forget he was a prancing muscle-bound ballet dancer with an accent plummier than a member of the English royal family sucking a bagful of plums, and started to think that not only was he a hardcore, gangsta-rappin' homeboy from the 'hood, he was a *star* to boot. Cue tantrums like the one we'd witnessed back at the oasis.

But why had me and Bentley been invited along, I hear you ask?

It turns out that Phones and the twins had been working on a new track for the album. It was going to be the killer track, the one that got the Phatphreak Crew noticed. The breakthrough tune. They'd got the main track down, enough to shoot the video in the desert (I tried to tell them that whole desert video thing was *old*, but they chose to ignore me).

They'd been stuck on finding what they called the hook to this killer track. Fluff had wanted to use a loop of Cleopatra (his revolting cat) but the other Phatphreakers hadn't been too enthusiastic about having a pussycat (and a real fluffy one at that) on their track. They had just decided to go with it anyway when we'd turned up and Bentley had done his mighty thunder bark thing. Phones had taped it and sampled it into the mix. With our authentic street-cool barks added to the pot, they were convinced they had the makings of The Next Big Thing to hit the gangsta rap scene and we'd been invited to join the Crew on the rest of their tour.

"Kinda like a mascot-type arrangement," said Phones.

"But with no money," said Freddie, hastily, a worried look passing over his little Scottish face, like a cloud. We nodded and he relaxed. Just escaping was good enough for us. Still, Freddie had us make some pawmarks on a hastily

drawn-up contract. I didn't understand much of it, but it seemed to say that Freddie and the Phatphreakers owned our barks for the rest of eternity, on every bit of the earth and on any planets yet to be discovered. We signed anyway – what do we know? We're dogs.

Fluff Booty wasn't happy with our invite.

"Tha's BLEEP," he said. "I don' figure on this track more than but a coupla shouts. How come these mangy BLEEPS get top billin'? Ain't right. The fans want me, not two BLEEP BLEEP talentless hairy BLEEP BLEEPS. Plus, I thought we was gonna use Cleo's tones on the track? Now we usin' these BLEEP BLEEP mutts? I gotta get me my agent."

Freddie reminded Fluff that he was his agent and oiled some soothing words in his direction. It didn't seem to do much for his disposition but he quietened down eventually and sat scowling at the back of the bus with his girlfriend, a woman with a face like a bee-stung vampire, and his fat moggy. With my super-doggy hearing I could hear him practising his street slang like an actor practising his lines.

"They's disrespekin' me. No one's checkin' for Fluff Booty. I's dope fool, you listenin'? I is dope, the reel deel, *word*. Yo dawg, meet ma homies, y'all slam by my … oh gosh Prunella, what is that damned word they use to describe their grisly little houses? What? Oh, of course, 'crib', thank you so much. Yes, y'all slam by my *crib*, put some cow on the grill, happenin'…"

I tuned his prattle out and turned to more important matters: food. Me and Bentley celebrated our escape from those military dudes by polishing off the rest of the Scooby snacks.

"You think they've given up?" I asked.

"Nope," said Bentley. "But they might find it harder to follow us now we're part of the Phatphreak Crew."

I settled back into the plush. What with all the excitment we'd been through I figured my jangled nerves were far too tightly wound for me to get much sle—

I woke up twelve hours and two states later with a mouth like the waste bag on a rotary sander.

The bus had stopped and everything was dark, inside and out. The Reverend Bentley was softly snoring away next to me. I stretched luxuriously and hopped down off the divan. The bus was deserted. Deserted in the desert (arf arf!). Outside the windows I saw the neon glow of a roadside diner with a big red sign shaped liked an arrow sitting on its roof that read *Desert Diner* and pointed directly down at the building.

The Phatphreak Crew must have stopped for refuelling and, now I came to think of it, I was feeling a trifle peckish myself, don't you know?

First things first, though: after twelve hours in the sack I felt the urgent need to take care of some important business. I pressed the door release button and it slid soundlessly back. The cold desert air rushed in and I stepped out on to the sand-blown road. Black clouds scudded across a vast inky sky and the desert wind whistled eerily past the tour bus, rocking it gently on its springs. The looming black shapes of saguaro cactus sat spookily out in the darkness, holding their arms up like they were directing traffic.

From my extensive research in the field of late-night trashy movies, I knew that the desert at night was positively infested with radioactive mutant ants, fifteen-metre spiders and monster aliens and suchlike. It was practically Times Square for freakoids out there.

But when a dog's gotta do what a dog's gotta do (or try at least)... I hunched into the night breeze and looked around for a private spot to do my biz. The large yellow streak running down my spine informed me not to head out into the desert, so I opted to toddle round the back of the diner where the lights cast a welcome glow for a few metres into the dark. An old dumpster sat five metres back from the rear door of the diner and I decided that was as good a place as any. I sat in the shadows and contemplated nature (keeping my eyes peeled for any signs of mutant-alien desert monsters, naturally). I sat and waited. And waited.

Now I'm not one of those dogs who usually has a problem getting the old digestive system to work. I don't want to boast but I'm about as regular as any pooch on the planet; when it comes to number twos, I'm number one. But something wasn't happening, and I remained as firmly blocked as if my ass had been encased in concrete.

I gave it up as a bad job and tiptoed over to the strip of light coming out of the open kitchen door. I always like to check the lie of the land before going into strange places; besides, maybe because I was out here in the middle of nowhere, I was as jumpy as a moggy in a microwave.

At the door I jumped on to a trash can set next to the wall and peeked in. The usual clattering sound of dishes and cutlery clanked through the steamy rectangle of light. The cook rushed from grill to serving hatch, sweat running down his face, and a plaintive country tune oozed out of the diner before being snatched away on the desert wind. I caught glimpses of some of the

Phatphreak Crew swilling coffee and eating large plates of brown greasy food. Phones was talking out the side of his mouth to the big twins and saying something funny about someone in the diner. He jerked his thumb over his shoulder and they all laughed. I peered in the direction of Phones' thumb and got an unpleasant sensation in my stomach.

No, no! Not that. I mean that I *saw* something.

Four guys, to be precise. They sat in a booth at the diner wearing military-looking black and serious expressions. They were looking with disgust at the Phatphreak Crew and drinking coffee.

It was the Relentless Posse, the Men In Black – they'd found us!

This news did nothing to ease my nerves and I prepared to make a run for it. Then I realized that if the Relentless Posse *had* found us, we'd be back in the clink, or worse, by now. I needed more information before I could form one of my globally famous cunning plans. I padded noiselessly to the kitchen diner; unless you count me tripping over the steel bucket and empty beer bottles some fool had left right in my path. It made no difference; the noise from the *Desert Diner* masked everything. As the country juke whined about his gal dying from a rare form of over-eating, I craned my neck as close as I could to check out the lie of the land. The three guys were still there, sitting ramrod straight in their booth… Wait a minute. *Three* guys? Where was the fou—

From out of the blackness, a hand latched on to my neck and I almost fainted with shock.

"GOTCHA!" said a voice in my ear, and then everything went black.

Chapter 7

Nighthawks at the Diner

"Pixies dance around the skypole, tra-la-la! Flax my mittens with bars of soap and iron the diamonds in my mother's sheets..." The first thing I noticed when I came to was that some fool was talking gibberish. It was me.

Something huge loomed above me and blocked the light.

"You fainted," said Bentley. He hoisted me upright. "Musta been the shock. You usually get so uptight?"

"I thought *you* were one of *them*!" I hissed. "One of the Relentless Posse. There's one missing!"

I pointed inside the diner. "See?"

Bentley looked inside. "I see four dudes there, brother. You sure you OK?"

"Well, of course there are four of them *now*," I said, my cool a trifle ruffled. "But there were only three of them wh – Oh forget it."

"Why are they so interested in us?" said Bentley. "It's not like we've got anything of theirs. Not since Rover wiped out."

"Never mind *why*," I said in an urgent whisper. "The important thing is that they're *here*, and they're looking for us, and it's only a matter of time before they catch us! We gotta go!"

I tugged at Bentley's arm. For all the effect I was having I might as well have been pulling at a hairy version of Stonehenge.

"I dunno," he said slowly, rubbing his snout. "We make a break now we're back to square one. And what chance do we have out in the desert?

At night? No, my plan would be to ride this one out, see how it plays."

Inside the *Desert Diner,* the Relentless guys had finished slurping coffee and were moving around the Phatphreakers showing photos of something.

"See?" I said. "They're asking about us! Someone's gonna spill the beans, you big doughnut!"

Bentley looked at me sadly.

"Nonsense!" he said. "Have a little faith, brother! And don't disrespect me again, y'hear? It's not nice."

A mighty paw shot out and cuffed me playfully. I shot back about eight metres towards the dumpster.

Fortunately my head broke my fall and, apart from what felt like a couple of broken ribs and a few loose teeth and a piercing, knife-like pain down my entire right side and a buzzing noise between my ears, I was OK.

Bentley was still peering into the diner. I brushed myself down and tiptoed back over. Inside, I could see Phones looking at our pictures as one of the Posse stood next to him. Phones shook his head and passed the photo back. I could see Slim and Shady doing the same. Freddie hesitated, but a stern glance from Phones and he too shook his head. It looked as though the Phatphreak Crew were helping us out.

And then I saw Fluff Booty.

He was at the end of the counter, blowing the froth off a cappuccino. Cleopatra sat next to him, her nose in the air and her tail moving slowly from side to side. One of the Relentless guys gave him a card and then thrust our photo under his nose. Fluff Booty scowled at the guy, giving him his best pretend ghetto stare. It had no effect and the guy just pointed at the photo again. Fluff glanced at it and his face lit up. The agent noticed and perked up.

"This is it, bro'," I whispered to Bentley.

Just as Fluff was about to speak, Phones appeared next to him, reaching over for the sugar bowl. He jogged Fluff's arm and upended his cappuccino. The hot coffee splashed into Fluff's lap and he leaped from his stool whooping and howling. Cleopatra leaped on to the counter and hissed. Phones looked straight across at us and flicked his eyes in the direction of the bus. We got the message and raced around the side of the diner. The bus doors were standing open and we jumped aboard, our hearts pounding.

At the back of the bus and over to one side were Fluff's personal quarters, and we dived straight in through the red velvet drapes.

"Woah!" exclaimed Bentley stopping short.

Most of the space was taken up with Fluff's huge, zebra-print waterbed. Every centimetre of the bed and every centimetre of every other surface was taken up with fluffy toy animals. They gazed at us blankly, looking more than just a little scary in the shadows.

"Guess we know why he's called Fluff," I said. Behind us we heard movement. People were coming out of the diner and were heading for the bus.

"Quick!" said Bentley, grabbing my arm. "In here!"

He bounced across the bed and tried to hunker down amongst the toys. I propped an enormous giraffe up against him and put a big pink pig on the other side. He still looked like a big old dog hiding amongst some stuffed animals. I looked around and scooped up a feather boa that was hanging on a nearby hook. I draped it around Bentley's neck and finished it off with a big floppy hat. It would have to do.

"You look simply adorable," I simpered.

"You breathe a word of this to anyone," growled Bentley, "and it'll be the last breath you ever take. Understand?"

I nodded, hardly listening. The noises were getting closer.

"SEARCH THIS BUS? I don't care what kind of X-File nonsense you BLEEP BLEEP BLEEP at me! You ain't got the jurisdiction to SEARCH THIS BLEEP BUS! You heard me: you can't *SEARCH THIS BUS!*"

It was Phones. He was letting me know what was about to go down. I rummaged deep down into the pile of toys, shoved a particularly vile bunny wabbit toy on to my head and let myself go limp. It wasn't hard, the adrenalin was pumping so fast my legs felt like sticks of jello. I forced my breathing to slow and got my heart rate down to a manageable gazillion jillion beats per minute.

The sound of boot-heels on the bus floor. Things being moved. Phones and Freddie arguing with the agents. I never heard them reply.

Then, a hand reached in and pulled back the drapes to Fluff's bedroom. I made my eyes stare straight ahead and I swear my pulse stopped. There wasn't a sound from Bentley. I couldn't see exactly what the black-clad agent was doing; he was just at the edge of my vision. I couldn't risk a glance. He stood for what seemed like a couple of centuries. I could feel my air running out and I was certain we had been rumbled.

The agent made a grunt of irritation and let the drapes fall back. The footsteps moved off and I let out a breath. Bentley did the same and his feather boa ruffled in the breeze. The sounds in the bus grew quieter and we heard the engine start. The Reverend put his paws together and looked upwards.

We'd been saved.

CHAPTER 8

Viva Las Vegas

We let a few minutes pass before pulling back the drapes and sticking our heads out. Phones was sitting opposite and burst out laughing. I couldn't figure out why until I glanced at Bentley.

"Take the duds off, dude," I said.

He growled and snatched the hat and boa off himself and threw them back into Fluff Booty's bedroom. Bentley looked at Phones and he stopped laughing. He held his hands up.

"OK, I'm sorry, dog. Just you looked kinda funny, s'all." Phones looked at us. "So," he said. "You guys are on the lam, huh?"

We didn't say anything. He wouldn't have understood anyway. Or maybe he would; Phones seemed like a real switched-on dude ... for a human.

He continued talking, anyway.

"Well, you can hang with us anyhow, at least till the gig in Vegas. We're outlaws too, right? Well, sorta." He stopped and looked right at us. "You musta freaked out some serious people though. Those X-Files BLEEPS were not from any dog pound. They's some kinda Special Forces BLEEPS. No identification stuff on them, all dressed in black camos, mirror shades, the full works."

We didn't say anything – when in doubt play dumb.

Phones had a round metal box in his hand and he held it out for us to look at.

"Take a good look, boys! This is our passport to the big time, my canine brothers!" He paused dramatically and spun the box on his finger. "The master tape of da next smash from da Crew, *Bark It Up!*"

We barked our approval and watched Phones stash the tape in a trunk covered in pink leopardskin. Then he flipped open a tiny cellphone and left us to our own devices. I noticed Fluff and Cleopatra watching us from across the bus as Fluff's girlfriend sponged coffee off his leather pants.

The Reverend and I trotted to the back of the bus and looked out into the desert night. He looked troubled.

"What's the problem, Reverend?" I asked. "We got nothing to worry 'bout, now. Next stop Las Vegas!"

"I'm not so sure," said Bentley. "Those Men In Black don't look the givin' up type, if you know what I mean."

I settled down uneasily and fell asleep.

The sound of the airbrakes going on jolted me awake. We had arrived at the city for the next Phatphreak Crew gig: Vegas!

Nine a.m. and the place was packed. Huge boards crammed with a million lightbulbs flashed screaming messages out at us: WIN! WIN! WIN!, ALL YOU CAN EAT! (I liked the sound of that one), PLAY TIC-TAC-TOE WITH A LIVE CHICKEN!

The hotels were gigantic. One was shaped like an Egyptian pyramid,

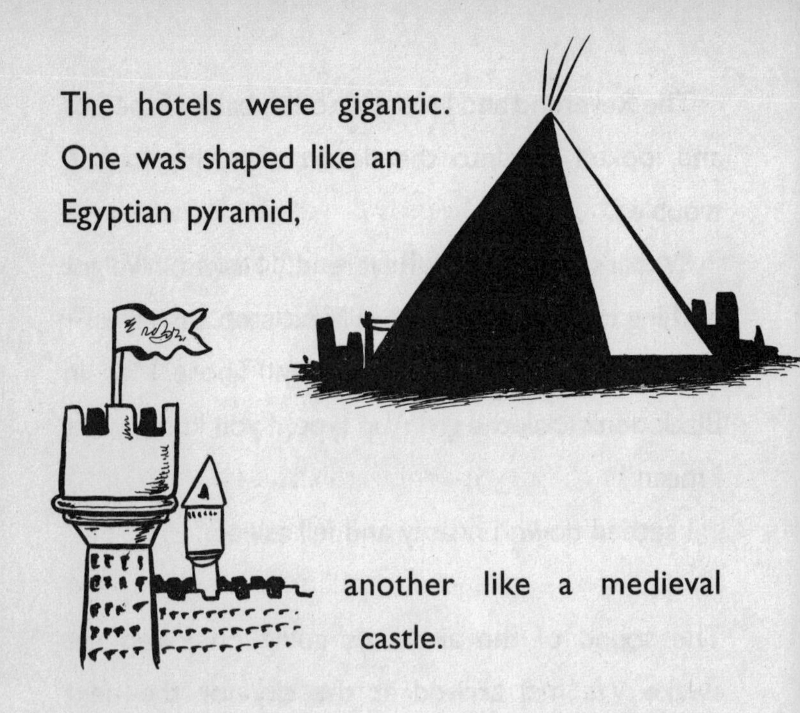

another like a medieval castle.

One hotel had a rollercoaster looping in and out of the building like some freaky giant had gone nuts with a can of Crazee String.

I could hear the tourists screaming as they looped the loop over Las Vegas Boulevard. TV screens the size of houses played music videos to the rush-hour traffic which was dotted here and there with stretch limos in white and black and gold and silver. The place was a head-scrambler and no mistake.

Even in the dry morning sun, the neon bit into my eyes like multi-coloured needles. (Did you like that bit? Very poetic, I thought.) I saw a huge lemon-yellow neon bone flashing on and off above a casino called *The Dog's Dinner* and felt right at home.

The bus pulled off the famous Las Vegas strip and headed down Tropicana Avenue to the gig. After a few minutes we drew up in a dusty parking lot outside a square concrete building with no windows. It was painted bright red and was called *The Pit.* The sign for *The Pit* was made in such a way that it appeared that the letters were on fire. I don't mean they were painted that way: real flames licked hungrily around the base of the lettering which hung crazily above the main entrance to the club. You could still make out the old sign under the new paint: *Tony's Spaghetti Lounge*, it read.

We all jumped down off the bus and stood scratching our asses in the frying-pan heat. It was only early but Vegas was already hotter than a chihuahua's chilli. *Ay caramba!*

A huge fat dude wearing a tropical shirt and eating a cream pie emerged from the main entrance, and told us all to come on inside outta da sun, what were we, morons, or what? We didn't need to be asked twice and we scooted gratefully inside. The fat guy shook hands with Freddie and nodded at the band.

"I'm Lennie. Lennie Fortelli. I'm da guy you spoke wit' last mont'. Dat da band?" he said, wiping the sweat off his brow with a handkerchief that could have made a sail for a fair-sized yacht.

Freddie nodded.

"Dey don' look like no ban'," said Lennie doubtfully. "Still whadda I know about it, eh?

If it ain't Tony Bennett or Ole Blue Eyes, fuggedaboutit. If it makes the punters happy, it makes Lennie happy, an' if it makes me happy then Big Tony is happy. And we all wanna keep Big Tony happy, you bedder believe it." He prodded Freddie with a meaty finger. "*Capeesh?*"

"Aye, yeah, er, Lennie," said Freddie. "We *capeesh*, OK?"

Now my eyes had had a chance to look around I could see we were in a large club. The stage jutted out into the auditorium. All around the stage were little tables with red plush velvet chairs, all laid out for dinner. Red velvet curtains hung down from the stage and the ceiling of *The Pit* was covered in twinkling fairy lights. A single spotlight on the stage picked out a stool with a microphone next to it.

An old-fashioned trilby hat hung on the mike stand.

As the team of roadies was already unloading the tour bus and ferrying piles of equipment into *The Pit*, Lennie stalked back into the shadows. Near to the bar area three other fat guys sat around a table playing cards. Lennie joined them and slipped into the empty seat. He said something and they all laughed.

Phones and the twins had stopped in front of the stage. Phones was looking around him in the manner of a man who suddenly finds himself on the surface of Mars.

"What the..." said Phones. "Freddie!"

Freddie looked up. "Hmm," he said.

"Don't play all innocent with me, you Scottish BLEEP BLEEP!" said Phones. "What is with all this red velvet Sinatra BLEEP? And who are those Soprano-lookin' suckers?"

At the mention of *The Sopranos*, Lennie and the other fat guys shifted around like bull seals on the beach. There were a lot of hand movements and scowls and then they took up the cards again.

There was a big pile of money on the table which was getting bigger by the minute.

While Freddie was soothing the Phatphreak Crew, me and Bentley watched Fluff Booty make an entrance, dressed from head to toe in shiny black leather with enough gold hanging round his neck to attract attention from any passing pirates. He was carrying Cleopatra (I was having a hard time stopping myself from catching up on my cat-whuppin' practice) and giving us The Look.

Bentley yawned and I let a little botty burp slip out; there was still something of a log jam down there, so to speak. Fluff turned on his white Nikes and loped off to the dressing room, a nasty little smile playing around his lips. I made my mind up to keep a special eye on the activities of His Bootyness and sloped after him.

Fluff went through a door around the back of the stage area. I followed and found myself in a long dark corridor. I caught a glimpse of Fluff's white sneakers up ahead as he turned a corner. Silently I slipped after him and watched as he lifted something from inside a large trunk covered in pink leopardskin. I recognized it straight away: it was the round metal box.

Our tape.

The only copy.

"Singing dogs!" spat Fluff. "What abolute tosh! One might as well skin a cat – oh, no offence, darling – and put that out for public consumption! Bah!"

I had a pretty good idea what Fluff Booty was up to. He was trying to sabotage our moment of glory.

"Five years at The Very Royal School of Posh Ballet and Theatrical Arts, to be upstaged by mere – *dogs*!" He shuddered. "I think not."

Fluff tucked the tape down the front of his pants. They were very baggy so he had plenty of room.

He scooped up Cleopatra, checked the coast was clear and headed back down the corridor. I could hear the clanking from his trousers as he passed, but with all that gold hanging round his neck I guessed that no one would notice. In any case, he didn't have the tape for long. I followed him back to his dressing room. Once there he closed the door and I could hear him hiding the tape. The door opened again and Fluff went back into the club. After a moment I darted into the dressing room.

Once inside it was the work of a moment to sniff out the stolen tape, thanks to the pong of Fluff's expensive hand lotion which led me to the hiding place as easily as if he'd painted it red and hung a sign on it. I picked up the tape and left.

Instead of turning back to the club I retraced my steps to where I'd noticed an exit to the parking lot. The Vegas sun streamed through and I emerged blinking into the baking heat. I could hear voices behind me and I panicked. I knew I had to hide the tape somewhere.

There was only one car in the lot, a big sleek black one with tinted windows. Somehow I thought it must belong to one of the card-playing guys. I slipped the lock (don't ask me how, it's a jailhouse secret) and looked inside. There was a large canvas bag on the back seat and I pushed the tape in there. I'd come back for it later.

I'd only just closed the door when the club door opened and Fluff Booty stepped out. He eyed me suspiciously so I cocked my leg against the wheel of the Merc and did what comes naturally (I wasn't having a problem with the waterworks). I'd have whistled if I knew how.

Fluff drew back his bottom lip in disgust. Cleopatra just looked at me blankly and I wondered for a moment if she was actually alive. The lights were on but there was definitely nobody home.

"Mangy cur," Fluff spat and turned back into the club.

I waited a few minutes then followed him inside. I needed to rest after all that excitement. Besides, tonight was our big night.

Inside the club I almost bumped into Fluff once more. He was speaking into a silver mobile phone and looking very sneaky. I tried to hear what he was saying but he clipped the phone shut with a sharp "snick" as I ambled innocently past. He gave me a sly smile which made me more than a little suspicious.

That guy was up to something else.

Chapter 9

Everybody in The House Go Boom

The gig was a sell-out.

Word of mouth amongst the ticket-scalpers on the Strip must have been hot, because we heard they were changing hands for top dollar. It should have made the Crew happy except for one small hiccup.

"What do you mean 'printing error'?" said Freddie.

Lennie Fortelli shrugged.

"What can I say? It's a freakin' printing error, OK?"

"No! It's not OK, Lennie!" said Freddie. "I mean, look at them!"

He turned and pointed through the stage curtains at the audience. The Phatphreak Crew audience was easy to spot. All baggy pants, gold chains, basketball vests and baseball caps. They stood ten deep, lined back against one side of the club. They didn't look happy.

"So?" said Lennie. "I thought that's what dose guys normally look like."

"Not them," said Freddie. He pointed to the other side of the club. "Them!"

Along the other side stood hundreds of cowboys and cowgirls. They too stood sullenly, arms folded, glaring across three metres of empty dancefloor at the Phatphreak Crew fans.

"I told ya," said Lennie. "It's a printin' error. They've come to see these guys." He flipped a thumb behind him to where an unhappy-looking band were tuning up. They were all wearing stetsons and glittery cowboy shirts.

"*The Texas Toetappers?*" said Freddie, reading a poster tacked to the wall.

Lennie nodded.

"They've agreed to go on first," said Lennie with a look on his face that spelled out he thought that was an end to the matter.

"Oh aye? Well, that's jest ticketyboo then, isn't it? On your head be it," said Freddie. "But I dinna like it and the boys ain't gonna be happy."

Lennie lifted Freddie up by the front of his shirt and jabbed a meaty finger into his chest.

"Listen, Braveheart," he whispered. "The last guy that spoke to me like that wound up not speakin', if you catch my drift. And I could care less about wedder or not 'the boys' like it. A deal is a deal. *Capeesh?*"

"*Si*, I mean yeah, OK," coughed Freddie. "You're da boss. I mean, the boss."

Lennie patted Freddie on the side of his cheek and put him down.

"I thought ya'd see it my way. Besides," he continued, "da Toetappers are Big Tony's favourite, and we don' wanna upset Big Tony, now do we?"

Freddie smoothed the front of his shirt and backed off. Lennie lumbered down the steps into the club. He still had a white napkin tucked under his chin. There were tomato stains all over it. As Lennie reached the back of the club and took his seat with the other big Italians, the lights dimmed and a voice came over the speaker system.

"Ladies and-a gennelmen! *Tony's Spaghetti Hou… The Pit* is proud to present, for *one* night only, straight from a month long residency at *Al's Chop House* in Flatville, Nebraska, the Lone Star State's finest: THE … TEXAS … TOETAPPPPPEEERRRSSS!!!"

The audience went wild. Well one half of them, at any rate. You can probably guess which half. The Phatphreak Crew fans stood open-mouthed as the curtains went back and revealed the Texas Toetappers in all their spangled glory. I think the first tune was called *My Gal Likes to Polka*. I didn't stay to watch. I was too scared.

"Let's check what's happening backstage," I suggested to Bentley. He nodded and we trotted away as the cowboys whooped and hollered.

I'd filled Bentley in on the incident with Fluff earlier and we'd decided to retrieve the tape after the gig and give it back to Phones. It wouldn't be missed until the Crew were back in the studio, and I didn't want to give Fluff another chance at ruining our shot at pop superstardom.

Freddie was having a tough time convincing the Crew to go onstage.

"We got a street rep, man!" said Shady. "How's it gonna look if we go on after the BLEEP BLEEP Texas Toetappers? I'll never be able to show my face in the 'hood again."

It was only by pointing out their choices that Freddie convinced the band. "He made me an offer I couldn't refuse."

"How so?" said Phones.

"We play, Big Tony lets us live," said Freddie. "We don't play, we sleep with the fishes, *capeesh?*"

We decided to go on.

An hour later, the Texas Toetappers had finished their set (a little confusingly, I thought) with a rousing rendition of *Sweet Home Alabama*. But the cowboys seemed to like it and they stamped their snakeskin boots and threw their hats in the air with plenty of hollerin' and whoopin' and all the other stuff that cowboy-types love to do. Then they all stomped off to the bar, bought beer and waited for the Phatphreak Crew to come on. I don't think they wanted to hear us but they were in the mood for trouble.

We waited in the wings as the Crew burst onstage with their anthem, *BLEEP the BLEEP BLEEP*.

The bass was so loud it shook the beer glasses on the cowboys' tables and rattled my teeth.

In a lull I could hear Lennie shouting, "Keep the goddam noise down, ya punks!"

The fans went wild. The Crew followed *BLEEP the BLEEP BLEEP* with *Straight Outta BLEEP BLEEP*. If anything this was even louder. Slim and Shady strutted the stage behind Fluff. I had to admit, once onstage he looked the part. He flexed his muscles and scowled at the audience from behind a pair of diving goggles. He wore these underneath a flowered shower cap. His pants were so baggy his knees dragged on the floor. I could see that he had three different brands of underwear on.

"This one goes out to all my homies out dere," said Fluff, tugging on the loose material at the front of his pants. "Dis one's for all da homies MIA."

The Crew launched into the opening bass notes of *Bark It Up!* and we realized that this was our Big Moment. Bentley gave me a reassuring smile and we bounded onstage. The place was pumping and me and Bentley strutted our stuff along with the rest of the Crew. It came to Bentley's turn to bark and Phones handed him a mike. Amplified, the roar sounded like one of those sonic booms that happens when a jet goes extremely fast.

Glasses shattered along the back of the bar and Lennie's plate cracked, sending hot spaghetti sauce all over his lap. Several of the cowboys' moustaches dropped straight out.

There was a moment's stunned silence and a sliver of broken glass tinkled as it fell to the floor. Then Phones kicked the bass back in and the place erupted. Even some of the cowboys were dancing. I did my bit and, while not as spectacular as the Reverend's stupendous effort, I thought it kicked *serious* ass. The crowd did too. Every time me or Bentley barked the crowd barked back too. Fluff scowled nastily from under his flower-patterned shower cap.

"We gotta hit!" yelled Phones to me, as we rocked up a Phat one. "Just listen to 'em!"

It was true. Every time we barked the audience howled. Some of them even got down on all fours and started doing a new dance.

"Man," said Slim. "Once they start inventin' dances you know you hit the sweet spot!"

I was having such a good time that at first I didn't notice something odd happening out in the audience. With stage lights glaring in our eyes we could only catch glimpses of the crowd. In the middle there were three heads moving. That was OK but, and here's what I should have cottoned on to sooner, they had no rhythm. They tried to look like they were part of the crowd but it was no use. They dibbed when they should have dobbed, they shimmied a coupla beats behind the bass line and they used their hands in a way no self-respecting rap fan would ever do. Frankly I was embarrassed for them.

I peered more closely. The three guys looked like the rest of the Crew fans, if a little taller:

baggy trews, vests, sports shirts, chains, baseball caps, shades – but something was a little "off". Then, with a shock, I realized who those guys were – it was the Relentless Posse (or three of them, at least). What was it with those guys?

What made me and Bentley, two street mutts with nothing except the fur we stood up in, so attractive (other than my wolfish good looks, that is)?

I looked to see if Bentley was checking this and saw Fluff grinning at me. Everything fell into place at once like a picture coming into focus. He'd grassed us to the feds, the stinking stool-pigeon! That call I'd heard him making backstage must have been to the Relentless guys. Now I thought about it I remembered seeing one of them slip Fluff a card back at the *Desert Diner*. Bentley had clocked it all too.

"We gotta go!" I yelled.

He nodded and pointed backstage. The fourth agent stood waiting in the wings, a slight smile on his face. He looked ridiculous in a white vest, gold chains and shiny black baggy shorts which reached down below his knees, but I still didn't want to get too near.

"Follow me!" I shouted to the Reverend and I stage-dived straight into the mosh pit that had formed at the front. The audience cheered and caught me on a sea of outstretched arms.

Bentley followed. We swam across the top of the audience towards the back of the hall. The knot of fans followed us preventing the Relentless Posse from getting near. Behind us the Phatphreak Crew kept the beat going.

"The door!" I yelled. "Let's go!"

We leaped down, pushed open the emergency exit and ran into the parking lot. The crowd surged around the door and, looking back over my shoulder, I could see the Relentless guys trying to get through.

"They won't be long!" said Bentley. "Let's go!"

I began to run towards the lights on the Strip when I remembered something.

"The tape!" I wailed. "We gotta give the master tape back!"

I raced around the parking lot looking for the big black car. It was still there and I breathed a sigh of relief. I did my trick with the window and jumped inside. The bag was still there, although it looked much heavier than I remembered.

"C'mon, brother," said Bentley. "They're coming!"

We looked and saw the three posse guys come out of the emergency exit. The fourth guy had come around the back in a pincer movement. The band had stopped playing and were out in the parking lot too.

"What now?" I hissed.

"There!" said Bentley. He pointed at a monster pick-up truck with huge oversize wheels that was backing out of a parking space about six metres away. One of the Texas Toetapper fans was leaving.

"Let's hitch a ride," said Bentley.

We sprang from the car and raced across to the truck. Bentley leaped into the back of the truck and held out a paw. Out of the corner of my eye I saw Lennie Fortelli turn purple as he saw the bag.

"What the –" he said, wiping sauce from his mouth (doesn't that guy ever stop eating?). "Gimme the bag, ya mutt!"

"Throw me the bag!" shouted Bentley. "We may need it to get out of this mess!"

I threw and the bag landed with a thump. The tape of *Bark It Up* flew out and flashed silver under the sodium lights before bouncing into the truck.

As Phones realized what it was his expression changed in a flash from warm to as cool as a polar bear's rear. "Hey, you stinkin' backstabbers! That's our BLEEP BLEEP master tape!"

He shouted something else about a "cap" and my "ass", but I couldn't hear it too clearly above the roar from the monster truck engine.

I tried to explain to Phones but it was no use, the driver of the truck was already turning out of the lot. Together with Slim and Shady, Phones was running after us yelling all sorts of threats. Behind them Lennie Fortelli wheezed a few steps in our direction before stopping and waving some of his bouncers after us.

"Big Tony's not gonna like this, ya lousy gonnifs!" he shouted between ragged breaths. "*Capeesh?*"

We raced out of the parking lot and bounced on to the Strip, the truck's massive tyres squealing on the hot asphalt. There was a good-sized rat pack chasing us: the Relentless guys, still looking stupid in their hip-hop disguises, Phones and the Crew, and Lennie Fortelli's guys. I waved and smiled and they all looked like they wanted to do nasty things to me. I didn't care, we were gone, home free...

Just then the truck screeched to a halt and the driver jumped down from the cab.

"Hey!" he said, looking at us. "Scram!"

I looked back and saw the mob gaining on us.

"Quick, Bentley!" I yelped. "Do something!"

Bentley leaped down from the pick-up and barged the cowboy out of the way.

"Forgive me, brother," he barked and jumped into the cab. He shifted into gear and put his paw to the metal. We screeched off leaving the cowboy wide-eyed in the dust. There was a blast from an air horn and he only just scrambled clear of a coachload of German tourists heading for *Circus Circus*.

"Dang!" he yelled. "A drivin' dawg!"

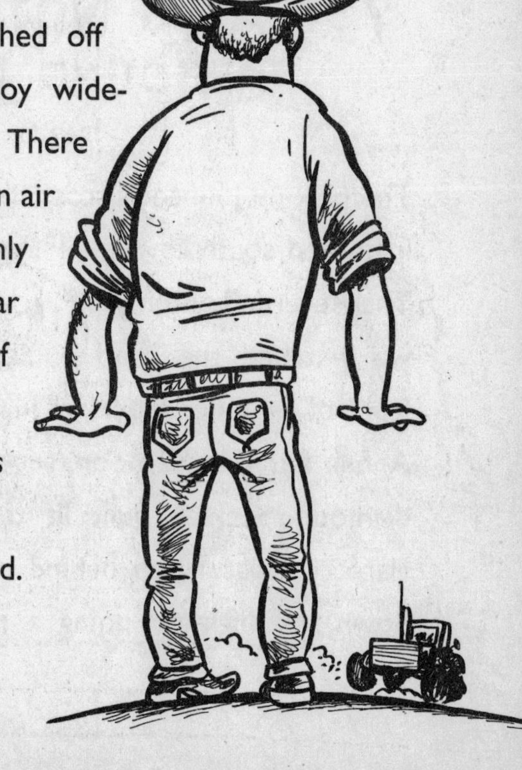

Chapter 10

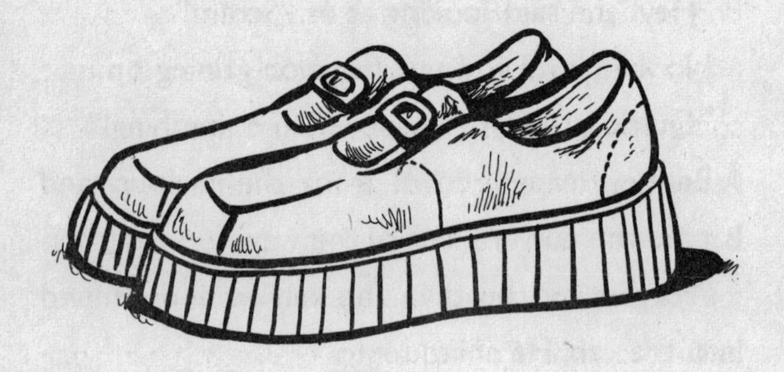

You Ain't Nothing But a Hound Dog

The pick-up jounced across the railway tracks as it headed south towards Phoenix (and Mexico!). The Reverend and myself jiggled up and down as we watched the road endlessly unravelling in front of us under a perfect high desert night sky. A full, fat, yellow moon set on a black velvet diamond-speckled quilt lit the desert up. The glare of Vegas faded behind us as we rocketed down the highway doing a nice safe 110mph.

I'll say this for Bentley; for a dog he sure could drive. He said he'd picked it up when he'd been a guard dog at a stock car stadium a few years back. Right now I was grateful because we dearly needed to put some serious miles between us and the Relentless Posse, not to mention Lennie Fortelli and the rest of Big Tony's mob. I'd checked in Lennie's bag and found a whole stack of money in there. It must have been the take from the gig. That explained why Lennie was so cheesed off about us taking it. Now I guessed that we were in Big Tony's bad books.

To top it off, the Phatphreak Crew were now on our tail as well. I hoped that we'd be able to explain to the boys that we weren't stealing the tape; it was just that right now wasn't the time. Bentley had another snippet of good news. "Don't forget we jacked this car, brother. We'll have the cops chasing us too."

"Oh, great," I said, slumping back against the seat. "And, let's face it, we won't be hard to spot. They'll just have to look for two dumber-than-usual dogs driving a monster truck."

Bentley looked at me thoughtfully. "What we need, my friend, is a disguise." He jerked a thumb through the back window of the truck. "Take a look back there and see what you can come up with."

I sighed but did as he asked and hopped through the rear window on to the bouncing surface of the truck's bed. I poked my head back through. "You couldn't slow down a speck?" I suggested.

Bentley grunted and stepped off the gas a little. We came down to a more sedate ninety-five. I looked around the truck and saw a big metal box lashed to the cabin. I flipped the lid and rummaged around. There were a lot of things I didn't recognize plus a guitar, a microphone and a whole stack of glossy flyers, the kind that small-time entertainers hand around to drum up some business. My eyes lit up.

"Hey Bentley," I shouted. "Pull over! I think we struck gold, pardner!"

Ten minutes later we were back underway, our brand new disguises in place. I was feeling very confident but Bentley wasn't so sure.

"This looks ridiculous," he snorted, looking at himself in the driver's mirror.

"A little less talk and a little more concentration," I replied as the truck drifted dangerously off line. I peeked in the mirror and admired my new sideburns and wig. "I think we look great."

Bentley snorted. "Is that right?" he said, a little sarcastically if you ask me. "Just how many people do you think are gonna be fooled by two dogs dressed as *Elvis* tooling down the highway? Don't you think the suits are a teensy-weensy little bit over the top for a truly convincing disguise?"

I glanced down at my white, rhinestone-studded jacket and pants. I'd become pretty attached to them in the last ten minutes. I looked *sharp*. I adjusted my new shades, brushed my wig into shape and curled my lip at my reflection.

"I think it'll do," I said. "Besides what choice do we have? At least wearing this we've got a chance when we pass through the next town."

Bentley made a noise like a constipated whale.

"Well?" I said huffily. "You got a better idea?"

"There's no need to sulk," said Bentley. "I'm wearing the stupid suit, aren't I?"

"Who's sulking?" I replied, folding my arms and sulking fit to bust. This was turning out to be one hell of a trip.

We drove through the night, blazing through tiny nowhere desert towns before hopping on to Route 66 and zipping through Kingman hunched low in our seats. Then it was out into the desert again and on towards the border.

I heard the choppers before we saw them. That old thock-thock thing again.

In front of us the dust blew across the road from the rotor-blade downdraught. There was so much dust Bentley could hardly see.

"That's one big chopper!" said the Reverend as the sound grew louder. I leaned out of the window and looked up.

It was, in fact, four, very different helicopters, all weaving in and out of each other and containing, in no particular order:

The Relentless Dudes, natch.

The Arizona State Police.

Big Tony's mob in a hired chopper.

The Phatphreak Crew in another.

It looked as though everyone had caught up with us pretty easily.

"Stop the truck!" boomed an amplified voice from the sinister black helicopter. "You have twenty seconds to comply."

"Pull over, bubba!" yelled another, this time from the Arizona cops. "You are driving a stolen truck!"

"I'm makin' you an offer ya can't refuse. *Capeesh?*" said the third.

"Give us our BLEEP BLEEP BLEEP BLEEP tape back, you BLEEP BLEEP little BLEEP BLEEPS!"

No prizes for guessing who that one was.

"Any bright ideas?" said Bentley. "Seein' as how you're the brains of the outfit an' all."

I ignored the note of sarcasm and concentrated hard. All I could think of was the smells coming through the windows: the smell of desert, cactus, hot city streets … I shook my head and tried to stop thinking like a dog.

Wait a minute. "City streets"?

"Put your foot down!" I yelled. "There's a city up ahead!"

Bentley looked at me but stamped down hard

on the gas pedal, wringing the last drop of speed from the truck. We crested a rise in the road and saw a city coming up towards us fast.

"Phoenix!" I shouted. "If we make it there we can shake 'em! They'll never be able to chase us this close to the city. They'll have to back off."

"You have ten seconds to comply!" said the metallic voice.

"Faster!" I yelled. I jumped in the back and started to throw things off the truck. Maybe we could get more speed if we were lighter.

I could see that Bentley had got the same idea and was eyeing me in a way I wasn't too sure about.

"Don't even think about it!" I said giving him The Eye.

"What?" he said innocently. "What?"

"You have five seconds to comply!"

Now we were driving past buildings and electricity pylons. There was traffic which frantically weaved around us as we careened across intersections and bounced over sidewalks.

An explosion ripped the ground up ahead of us and Bentley lurched the wheel to the left. We bounced heavily and landed back on the road.

"They're shooting!" I squealed.

"No kiddin'," muttered Bentley and gunned the monster truck, wringing every last ounce of speed from its engine.

The streets were getting more crowded with traffic and the buildings growing higher by the minute.

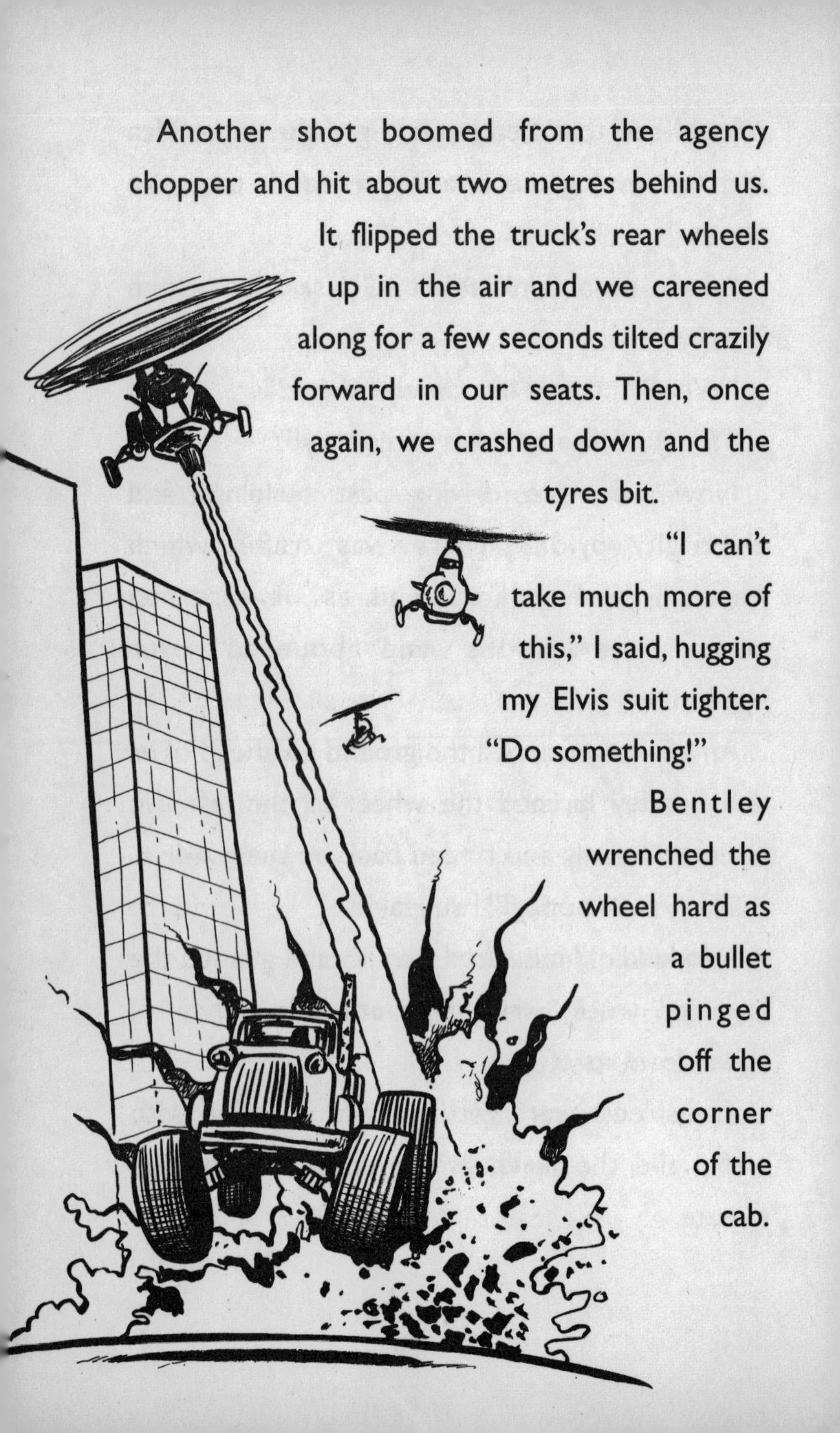

Another shot boomed from the agency chopper and hit about two metres behind us. It flipped the truck's rear wheels up in the air and we careened along for a few seconds tilted crazily forward in our seats. Then, once again, we crashed down and the tyres bit.

"I can't take much more of this," I said, hugging my Elvis suit tighter. "Do something!"

Bentley wrenched the wheel hard as a bullet pinged off the corner of the cab.

We screeched around the corner of an intersection and found ourselves facing a screaming, howling wall of traffic.

"AAAAAAAAARRRRGGGGHH!" someone howled. It was me.

We were barrelling down a one-way street the wrong way. A huge semi bore down on us and we were seconds from becoming Phoenix roadkill. There was nowhere to go. Either side of the semi was blocked. Bentley looked at me, shrugged and spun the wheel hard to the right. We lurched up on to two wheels and I got a flash of the helicopters rising into the air away from the crash that was about to happen. Phones winced. The Arizona cops talked into walkie-talkies, presumably arranging for someone to scoop our lifeless corpses from the baking tarmac. The Relentless guys I couldn't see.

We caroomed up on to the kerb, bounced over the sidewalk and smashed through a gigantic plate-glass window. There was a moment's silence as we flew through the air. A banner was strung across the room and we flew straight through it. People below scattered in blind panic as we hit the floor and spun round and round, the tyres squealing on a polished marble floor before coming to a rest against a gigantic abstract sculpture.

We staggered clear of the truck, brushing bits of broken glass and metal off our suits and wigs. I noticed Bentley had remembered to bring the bag with him. I patted the pocket of my Elvis suit and checked the master tape of *Bark It Up!* was still there. I looked at the crowd: there was something very familiar about the people standing around watching us.

I looked at the banner we'd ripped down.

Phoenix Conference Centre Welcomes the Friends of Elvis! it read.

Chapter 11

Riot in Cellblock No 9

There were fat ones, thin ones, long ones and short ones. There were Elvises dressed in black, white, pink and yellow. There were punky Elvises, futuristic Elvises, zombie Elvises, girl Elvises, baby Elvises, even one entire family of Elvises.

All the Elvises stopped what they were doing and looked at us.

We looked at them.

I could see that they were making their minds

up about us. On one hand we had crashed through the window, almost splattering them across the floor like so much Elvis jam. Plus we were kinda funny-looking.

On the other hand we *were* dressed as The King and it was this, I think, that finally won them over. They burst into a round of applause, obviously deciding we were part of the jamboree.

A large, late-period Elvis was standing on a raised platform at one end of the hall holding a microphone. "Well, uh, hey, let's have a big, lip-curlin' welcome for our two, er, *friends*!" he shouted into the mike. "Let's give 'em a hunk-hunka burnin' lurve! That was one mind-blowin', uh, entrance, thank you ver' much!"

The Elvises applauded and cheered.

We smiled and waved. Bentley even dropped to one knee and curled his lip, Elvis-style, and the crowd went wild, just as three of the Relentless agents swung through the broken window on the end of long ropes.

"I'm getting pretty ticked off at those dudes," I said. "Don't they have homes to go to?"

"Everybody freeze!" shouted one of them through a megaphone.

"Now, that ain't polite," said the Elvis on the mike. All the other Elvises burst out laughing and carried on shopping and browsing along the stalls and stands set out in the hall.

"I said, 'Everybody freeze'!" said the agent again, looking around. He was obviously used to bossing people around.

The Elvises were made of sterner stuff. All those years of growing sideburns and wearing rhinestone-studded jump suits must have toughened them all up because they carried right on ignoring the agent with the megaphone.

"Let's go!" I said pulling Bentley towards a door. We could hear the crisp crack of boot-heels racing after us as we crossed to the door. From another side of the hall I could hear the booming voice of Lennie as he urged his men to put us on ice.

The Arizona cops were coming from the other side. The door ahead was our only chance. Just then it opened wide and the Phatphreak Crew stood in our way. Phones took in the situation at once and I could see he was struggling. I reached inside my jacket and tossed him the master tape.

"Here!" I yelled. "I'll explain later!"

Phones caught the tape and smiled.

"Hey!" said Fluff Booty. "I demand an explanation – I mean, whass goin' down, bro'? This sucker ripped us the BLEEP off!"

Bentley barged Fluff out of the way as easily as if he'd been made of cotton candy. Cleopatra sailed high into the air, hissing and mewling, and we ran for it.

"We'll hold 'em off!" yelled Slim.

"Yeah!" yelled Shady.

I looked back and saw that the Crew might not be enough to hold off everyone.

"Wait!" I yelled. "I just thought of something!" I grabbed the bag from Bentley and ran up a set of steps leading up to a wide walkway surrounding the hall on four sides. At the top I leaned back and hurled the bag out into space towards the high-speed fans in the ceiling. The fighting stopped as everyone watched the bag sail out. Lennie went pale and clutched his chest. The bag hit the central fan and exploded as the high-speed blades ripped it open, cascading money everywhere, the bulk of it falling directly on to Fluff Booty.

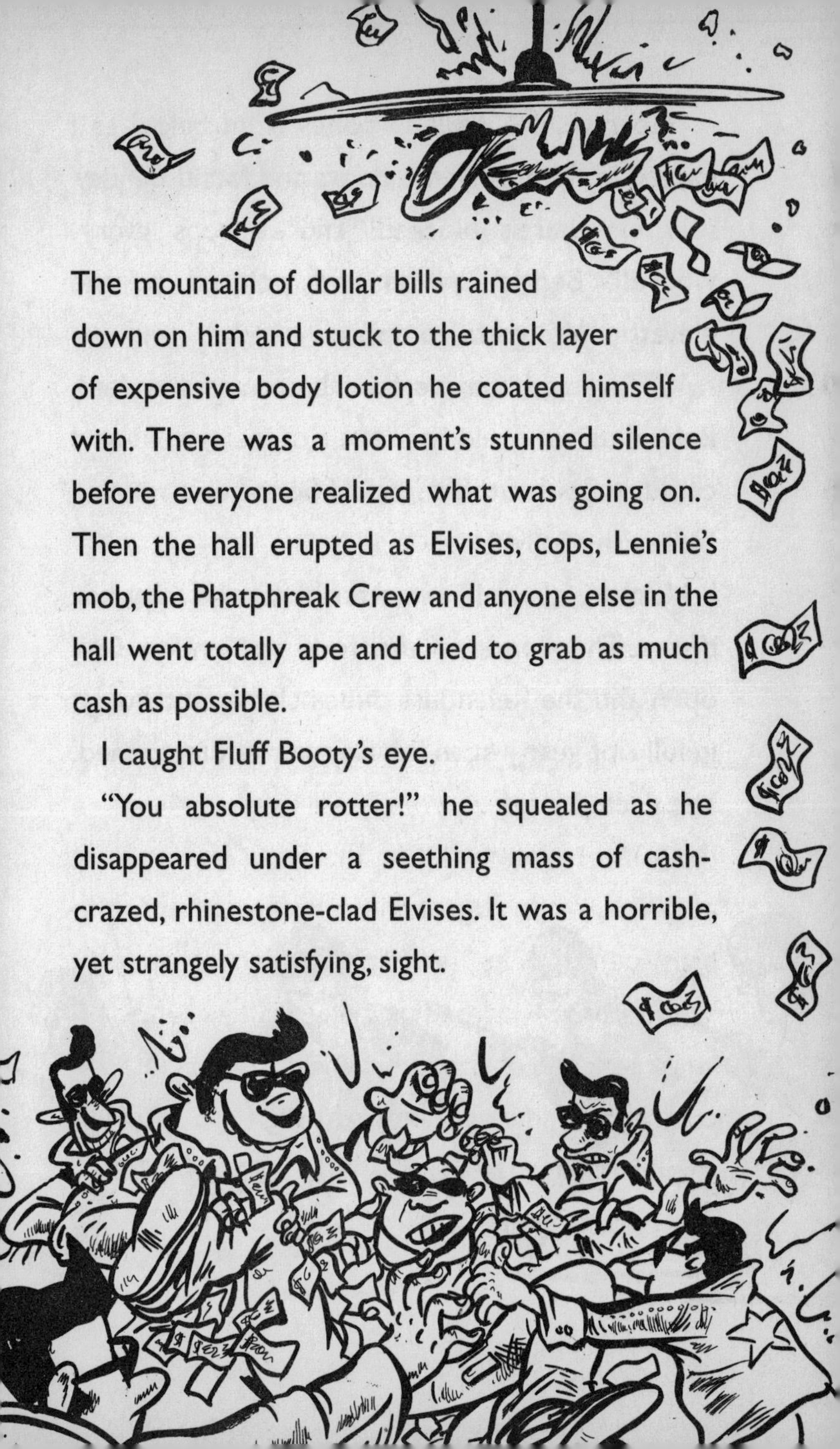

The mountain of dollar bills rained down on him and stuck to the thick layer of expensive body lotion he coated himself with. There was a moment's stunned silence before everyone realized what was going on. Then the hall erupted as Elvises, cops, Lennie's mob, the Phatphreak Crew and anyone else in the hall went totally ape and tried to grab as much cash as possible.

I caught Fluff Booty's eye.

"You absolute rotter!" he squealed as he disappeared under a seething mass of cash-crazed, rhinestone-clad Elvises. It was a horrible, yet strangely satisfying, sight.

"Go man, go!" yelled Phones from below as I barged back through the doors and found Bentley.

"Everywhere's blocked! There's cops everywhere!" Bentley yelled and pointed to the elevator. "We gotta go up!"

We pressed the elevator button and waited. Behind us we could hear the riot losing volume. I could make out the sound of boot-heels running across the hallway.

"C'mon, c'mon!" I muttered to the elevator doors. The doors to the Elvis convention flew open and the Relentless dudes clattered through in full riot gear just as the elevator doors opened. We darted inside.

"Quick! The button!" I yelled.

Bentley's huge paw jabbed at the elevator buttons and the doors hissed shut just as the first agent slammed against it. The elevator whirred and we shot upwards.

"Where to now, brother?" said Bentley.

"There's only one place left," I said, slumping against the side of the cabin. "The top."

There were more than seventy floors but it only took us a minute to reach the top. The doors opened and we slipped out. Bentley wedged a fire extinguisher into the lift doors so it couldn't go back down. A small flight of stairs led up and we barged out of an emergency fire door into the blinding Phoenix sun. We were on the roof. We closed the door and pushed a heavy air-conditioning vent against it.

"It'll only hold 'em for a time," said Bentley.

"I know, man," I said. "This is it. We never did make Mexico."

I walked over to the edge and looked down.

They were everywhere.

On rooftops opposite, and in the street below, were what seemed like thousands of agents, cops and soldiers. Helicopters buzzed overhead. It was a total cop fest.

"I can't believe it!" I said turning to Bentley. "All this for a couple of dogs!"

"There's gotta be more to it than that," said the Reverend, pacing the roof.

We racked our brains. It didn't take long and we came up with nothing.

"DOGS!" barked a voice through a bullhorn. "THIS IS YOUR FINAL WARNING! COME OUT WITH YOUR PAWS IN THE AIR AND NOBODY GETS HURT!"

Me and Bentley stood in the baking heat and looked at each other.

"Remember the river?" I said. "They thought they had us then, Bentley."

"That's true, brother."

"Let's jump," I said. "I ain't goin' back to jail."

"You reckon we can make it?"

"It's possible," I said. "Anything's possible. Besides we'll probably get shot before we hit the ground."

"You go left, I'll go right," I said. "In all the confusion they might miss."

Bentley looked at me for a moment. A large tear wobbled in the corner of his eye.

"It's been a blast, brother," he said. We hugged and then broke apart.

"Let's kick some ass!" I yelled and we sprinted for the edge of the roof. We were going out in a blaze of glory.

We were about three metres from the void when the building shook violently. I braked hard and skidded. My paws came to rest right at the edge of the roof and for a moment I teetered over the drop. Then Bentley yanked me back and we fell face down on to the hot asphalt, our heads poking out over the edge of the roof.

A shadow fell across us and I could hear a whole lot of commotion from below. I looked up and my heart made like a third-rate Russian gymnast and performed a series of cartwheels in my chest.

Hovering right above us was a huge, dark, metallic shape. It was like something out of a Godzilla movie.

"What the...?" I heard Bentley say as he stepped back from the edge.

We scrambled out of the way as the shape landed with a sound like a jet engine winding down. A gigantic head bent down close to us. It had big black sideburns, an oily quiff and a pair of shades the size of a Buick. The surface was smooth and slightly reflective but even with the Elvis get-up on there was something familiar about it.

"Woof," it said softly, and I looked more closely.

"Rover!" I yelped. "It's *Rover!*"

I looked up at him. Rover had somehow transformed himself into Elvis, right down to the cuban-heeled boots. He was a dead ringer, except for the fact that he was at least five storeys high and made from some weird sci-fi metal and could hover in mid-air.

"You've, you've ... you're BIG!" I said. "Very, very big. And you're Elvis. And you're not dead!" I notice things like that, you see.

"*This* must be why they wanted to find you," said Bentley. "Looks like Rover here has a few tricks up his sleeve, so to speak."

I was about to start asking questions when a missile exploded right next to us, blowing a huge hole in the roof.

"Later," said Bentley hoisting me aboard Rover. Another missile streaked towards us and I said my prayers.

Rover reached up a massive metal hand and swatted it out of the sky like a bug. Instantly, ten or more missiles were launched and Rover's paws went into blurry Jackie Chan super-speed, batting them all aside.

"Nice action," said the Reverend admiringly.

"Thank you ver' much," mumbled Rover/Elvis.

Rover/Elvis began to lift clear of the roof. Little blue ripples of electricity snaked along his neck and from deep inside him there came a low grumble. Below us the agents, police and soldiers let loose with all they had.

There was a brief flash from the top of Rover's head and instantly a shiny protective bubble sprang up all around the new improved Rover. Missiles, bullets, everything, just pinged harmlessly away as we rose up into the sky.

"So long, suckers!" I yelled as Rover shifted into double-stellar hyper-turbo-drive and we blasted off across the Arizona desert at the speed of sound, me and the Reverend swapping high fives and giggling fit to bust. The Deadly Duo had done it again, beaten the odds and triumphed. Yay for us!

Chapter 13

Dirty Old Egg-Suckin' Dog

After ten minutes of face-wobbling flight Rover levelled off at about 2000 metres and slowed to a steady 200 miles an hour.

I sat down heavily against what looked like an exhaust pipe and as I did my stomach gurgled, telling me to find a restroom pretty soon. I rubbed my stomach gingerly and wondered if I'd eaten something nasty … then it hit me – Rover's remote control! Back when we first crash-landed in the desert I'd swallowed the thing. It must still be blocking me up!

I told Bentley and he laughed.

"You mean all that time you had that thing stuck inside..."

"Yes, yes," I interrupted. "There's no need to go into details."

"So that's why Rover could get to us so easy," said Bentley. "And *that's* why all those dudes have been following us like a pack of wolves all this time; they need to get their little toy back."

There were holes in this story.

"How come those Relentless guys missed Rover after we buried him, if they're so smart?

And how come Rover here didn't just blast up at supersonic speed right away and pick us up? And how come he looks like Elvis?"

Bentley was about to answer when a TV monitor popped up out of nowhere and began to play a tape. It was a desert scene. It showed me and the Reverend burying Rover. Then it showed us leaving. Then it showed Rover underground (there must have been a nose-mounted camera or something). As we watched, Rover started to burrow into the earth. A tail-mounted camera showed the earth being replaced behind him. Then we switched to the desert again and the guys in black. They looked and dug around but couldn't find a thing. Then the TV went blank and zipped back down into a slot on Rover's back.

Bentley let out a long breath. "He musta laid low until he got all ... swelled-up and fixed an' all, and then come chasin' his pappy!"

I wasn't too happy being thought of as anyone's pappy, especially not a giant flying mutant-robot-pooch like Rover. Still, he/it had come through for us, and now we looked to be home free, sailing pretty.

"What about the Elvis thing?" I figured I'd have Bentley stumped with that one but he just laughed airily.

"I seem to remember you telling me that this Rover got pretty mixed up with all kinds of creatures in that laboratory; a bit of this kind of dog, a bit of that, right?"

I nodded.

"Well maybe a bit of chameleon got mixed up inside him too along with all the technical stuff, hmm? And maybe that's why he can change shape and disguise himself and why everyone's so keen to grab a hold of him. He musta changed into Elvis to blend in."

"*Blend in?*" I said. "A twenty-five-metre flying Elvis dog?"

"Yeah, I know," said Bentley, holding up his paws. "But it doesn't mean that the dude wasn't *trying* to blend. It's still a good theory."

"You might have a point," I said. "Now all we

gotta do is figure out how to fly this thing."

"I think he's flying us this time, brother. Just settle back and enjoy the ride."

The time passed pleasantly enough until I noticed that the setting sun was on my left-hand side. I'm no genius (what do you mean, you already noticed?) but even I knew that that meant one thing…

"We're going north!" I yelped, scrambling upright.

Bentley looked at the sun and nodded.

"Yep, sure looks that way, brother."

I looked down and started to recognize the landscape below me. My super-doggy sense of disaster was operating at max and my tail began to twitch.

"I'm getting a funny feeling about this taxi ride," I said.

"Jes' relax, brother," said the Reverend. "What can possibly go wrong now?"

Just then Rover slowed, and we started to glide down towards a large, gloomy-looking building. I knew right away what it was and where we were headed. My sense of doom had been 110 per cent accurate.

We were headed right back to Z-Block.

"Relax!" I shouted. "*Relax* he says! Sure, I'll relax myself right back into the slammer! Look!"

I began yelling instructions and pressing various rhinestones on Rover's back, but nothing happened. We drifted lightly down into the exercise yard at Z-Block, dogs scattering in every direction. Rover bent one knee and extended an arm towards the crowd of dogs and guards.

"Thank you ver' much," he said and promptly fell asleep.

Fester looked at us and smiled. It wasn't a pleasant sight.

"Well, well, well," he said. "Look what the cat brung in!"

And that just about brings our story up to date. After all our running, Rover/Elvis dumped us right back into the Pound. He showed no inclination to whizz us out of there again; in any case the remote was taken off me pretty plenty pronto by a squad of those black-clad dudes (What is it with secret military types and black clothes? Don't they ever want to see how a mint green or dusty pink might look?) who arrived at the Pound about ten minutes after we landed and took Rover/Elvis and the remote with them.

Bentley kept looking at me like I was responsible for the whole thing. How was I to know that Rover had been set on *Fetch* mode when we buried him, and that we were the thing he needed to fetch? In any case I think the Reverend was secretly quite relieved to be back inside. At least he could take off the Elvis disguise, which had been bugging him since Vegas. Plus I think he needed to be amongst his flock again; out on the street who knows what might have happened?

As for me, I didn't mind too much either, if truth be told. We had had one major, crazy rollercoaster ride over the past few days, but it was nice to not be getting chased every waking minute. The Phatphreak Crew released *Bark It Up*! and it screamed in at number one, what with all the publicity surrounding the Phoenix Elvis riot and the giant mutant flying Elvis dog episode. The guys came to visit and would have sprung me in a minute but, as Freddie helpfully pointed out, having a singer locked up in chokey did their street rep (and the sales of the record) no harm at all.

I also had a visit from Lennie Fortelli.

"Big Tony sent you a present," he said, handing me a fish wrapped in newspaper. "He said to make sure and look him up if you ever get out. He said if you don't you can count on him lookin' you up, *capeesh*?"

So here I am again, back in the lock-up, straight outta Z-Block, the Notorious B.A.D., King of the Rappers, locked up in the slammer, under the hammer, you know what I'm sayin', yo mama?

Oh, fuggedaboutit.